I0586895

A Hero in the Making

(book one)

By Simon Woods
Illustrated by Ralph Platt

Dedicated to my wonderful daughters;
Molly and Tilly.
You're the best, and in my thoughts every
second of every day.

Special thanks to;
Ben Tuffs, Stephanie and Emily Paice, and Megan Owens, for their enthusiasm and help. But I also have to mention, without a doubt, Chris Debenham and Dave Judd for their comments and for putting up with me. Without their help and encouragement Brave Dave would have remained just a figment of my imagination, and would have never appeared in print.

Chapter 1
The Written Exam

The top of a fairly large rocky hill poked above
the swirling grey mist. The moon shone down
from a sky that was always night. And the
moonlight reflected off the slate tiles that made
up most of the roof of the stone and castle-like
Poltergeist University. The other parts of the
roof were made from holes, to the annoyance of
the university's staff who happened to live in the
attic; each of whom got especially annoyed
when it rained.

All this, the Poltergeist University, the holes and the rain, lived in a placed called the Netherworld; a place where the mysterious creaks at night, the weird noises from the dark, and other ghostly and ghoulish things lived, until they were old enough. After that they had to make a living in the real world—our world— the world of mums and dads, of babies and grannies, and, of course, the world of that annoying brother or sister who were sometimes okay.

Along a large dark oak panelled corridor glided a large black cloak with a very high black collar. The interesting thing about the collar was not how tall it was, nor the fact it pointed up instead of down, the interesting thing was that contained within the collar's semi-circle was nothing, no neck and no head, it was one of the reasons the Headless Master had given up trying to wear a tie. After the three hundred years of receiving a tie for Christmas, from his daughters, he'd decided it must be some kind of joke they'd been playing on him for all that time, so he'd stopped bothering.

Out of his cloak's sleeves long grey-green forearms hung. Attached to the arms were two huge hands with fingers of a very pointy nature. In one of the pointy-fingered hands was a sheath of papers, it was the written exam paper for GCSE (**G**hostly **C**ertification in **S**caring

Everyone), **G**eneral **H**aunting of **S**choolkids and **T**eachers, (GHoST) Module 1 of GCSE Poltergeistdom.

As the Headless Master glided towards the lecture hall he knew he was getting nearer. Although he'd been at Poltergeist University on the Rock for some time now the very nature of this ethereal academy meant that in-school routes changed, sometimes just because they could and other times because the wind was blowing from a particularly difficult direction and the halls had become filled with fog—now was one of those times.

With his free hand he pulled his bat-nav out of his pocket after a few moments it flapped its wings as he waved it from left to right in front of him, and then it squeaked. The Headless Master nodded to himself and put it back in his pocket; the noise of the Movitalls, the young pre-graduate poltergeists, and his bat-nav confirmed he was still going in the right direction.

The Headless Master came to a halt outside of lecture hall 101 and tried to shake his head in dismay, which failed as it always did. These young Movitalls seemed not to have a care in the Netherworld. GHoST Module 1 was an extremely important exam to pass. He wondered how he could try to give them some idea of its importance. Then he smiled to himself and curled up into a small ball of black mist and popped through the room's keyhole, unseen, into the classroom.

Inside the lecture hall the young grey, gangly legged Movitalls, with oval heads and wispy green hair curled into a point, were doing young Movitall type things. Some were throwing folded up pieces of paper which glided to the front of the classroom, others were flicking the end of wooden rulers against the head of their classmate sat at the desk in front of them, which one would assume would be pretty pointless because they were, essentially, ghosts, but this being Poltergeist University the ruler always struck home with a slap or crack noise much to the annoyance of the student on the receiving end.

None of them noticed the small black ball of mist drop to the floor from the keyhole and roll towards the back of the lecture hall.

A few of the Movitalls sat at their desks in silence very worried about the exam and whether they'd pass it or not.

The Headless Master reach the back of the hall and inhaled; within seconds he was back to his normal size, but still none of the student poltergeists noticed.

The Headless Master inhaled again, this time not to expand himself, but to have enough breath for what he was about to say.

"MOVITALLS!" bellowed the Headless Master

"MOVITALLS!" he bellowed and the room shook, dust fell from the brick arches supporting the hall's ceiling. "SILENCE NOW."

Silence descended instantly. The Movitalls cowered in their seats.

"You see what I did there? Huh?" The Headless Master managed to give the impression he was looking about the room at each and every one of the Movitalls individually. "You don't learn to become this scary without taking your exams seriously. UNDERSTOOD?"

The room nodded in unison.

"Good. I am now going to handout the GHoST Module 1 written exam paper. DO NOT turn it over until I give the instruction. IS THAT

CLEAR?"

Again the room nodded in unison. The Headless Master walked around to each desk and placed on each an exam paper face down. Then he made his way to the front of the classroom and sat down in a high-backed wooden chair. On the desk was an hourglass filled with sand.

"Okay Movitalls, turn your papers over." The Headless Master inverted the hour glass timer and the sand began to flow from the top to the bottom.

"You may start," the Headless Master declared.

* * *

All too quickly the sand in the timer ran out and those Movitalls that had been keeping an eye on it sighed an unhappy sigh.

"STOP WHAT YOU ARE DOING," the Headless Master said as he stood up. "The written exam has finished."

There was a rustle of papers and the sound of pens being placed back on the desktops.

"I am going to collect your papers and you shall remain here, IN SILENCE, until the papers are marked. At this time I shall come back and notify those of you that have failed as you will not be allowed to take the practical examination. The marking process should take no more than 20 minutes."

Chapter 2
Announcement of the Practical
Exam

As the Headless Master walked back down the
corridor to examination room 101 he would
have smiled, but the fact he'd accidently lost his
head in his youth put an end to that. He could
have conjured a smiley face to appear in the air,
being the Headless Master of Poltergeist
University on the Rock, but smiling inwardly was
enough for him. He pushed the lecture hall's
large wooden door open and walked in, then

made his way to the desk at the front of the classroom.

"Okay, you young Movitalls," he started, "you have completed your written exam paper."

There was silence in lecture hall 101 as the Movitalls waited for their results to be read out by the Headless Master.

"I am very pleased," the Headless Master continued, "to say that this is the first year that...," the Headless Master paused for effect. "YOU HAVE ALL PASSED," he boomed finally and the room shook with his words.

"Woooooo, wooooooo, wooooo," the Movitalls cheered in a low ghostly manner.

The Headless Master let the gathered

students become silent before he carried on in a more serious tone.

"However, all that said, and congratulations to you all," he conceded, "it is one thing to pass a written paper sitting in a lecture hall, but it is totally something else to apply what you have learnt, in the world of the non-deceased. And it is this, the practical exam, which you will have to pass so that you may attain gainful employment as a fully-fledged poltergeist in the community of the non-deceased.

"My advice to you all is; don't celebrate now but prepare. The day for the practical exam will be All Hallows Eve, and will last two days. Remember one thing, young Movitalls, the

Masters of the Netherworld will be monitoring you during your exam. SO NO CHEATING." The Headless Master of Poltergeist University let the point sink in. "Okay, devil's luck to you all. Class dismissed," he said finally.

One of the Movitalls reluctantly raised its hand.

"Class, sit back down. It appears Nigel has a question and if that's the case then it could well be important to all of you."

The rest of the class moaned an eerie moan but sat back down anyway.

"Okay, Nigel, what is it you want to know?"

Nigel looked around feeling very conspicuous and apparent. "Erm," he mumbled.

"Speak up, I'm sure everyone is waiting to hear your question."

Nigel looked around the classroom once more, then swallowed and continued. "Why is our practical exam always on All Hallows Eve?" Although Nigel had expected the rest of his class to laugh at his question, no one did; it seemed they were curious as well, but had never had the courage to ask.

"I am surprised this simple question has never been taught," the Headless Master said. "As you all know the GHoST modules are exams all about how we present ourselves to the living so that we will always succeed in scaring them. Some of you will continue to go on to study further, if you succeed in the practical exam, and then start learning the techniques for scaring all adults, not just teachers, and those in schooling; for example, the children from kindergarten.

"Just to explain; a living person, who has a child, would not be able to live a normal life if that child just went to sleep every night. We contribute to the living's life style by making sure that their children seek recognition even when their need for food has been fulfilled.

"But to answer Nigel's question; All Hallows Eve, or Hallowe'en, is the day that most of the living celebrate the un-alive and the spirits of the un-alive. And this is why the GHoST module

2 exam is on *All Hallows Eve*—it's the time that all of us are able to interact with the non-deceased, those not like us, when, at other times, only the graduates and the trained can influence what happens in the world of the non-deceased."

"Thank you, Headless Master," Nigel replied.

"You're welcome. Anyone else?" the Headless Master asked. The rest of the room remained silent. "Okay then; class dismissed."

The Movitalls got up and left the lecture hall thinking about what they'd been told, wondering what the practical exam would likely entail.

Chapter 3
From Lightning a Life is Born

It was Friday the 31st of October, Hallowe'en in fact, and Jonesy was rounding up his flock of swans, getting them ready so he could take them somewhere warmer for the winter.

This was his job as he was the boss, not that he'd been voted in or anything. For some unknown reason, after he'd arrived and suggested the idea to the swans during their dinner, they'd said, "Honk."

Unfortunately for Jonesy his knowledge of

Swan-lingo was very basic and he took their response to mean 'okay', when in fact all they'd said was, 'What?' At the time he hadn't known swans couldn't hear whilst they were chewing.

Although Jonesy had joined their flock he was no type of ordinary swan. There was something about his little beady eyes, his hooked yellow beak and huge talons on his feet that made him stand out from the rest of the flock. In fact he was more of an eagle than a swan, and a big one at that. But not one of the swans in the flock had taken the time to explain this to him; mostly swans tended to be disinterested unless they had little'uns running around.

As spring, summer and autumn had packed their bags and left winter mooching about in what could only be described as a serious moody, Jonesy decided it was time to get going and take his flock off to Africa and warmer climes.

Their home at the lake was no longer a nice place to be—the worst of the British winter had arrived.

Not just winter but the weather itself was revolting. Blacker than black clouds blotted out the deepening blue of the early evening shedding huge drops of water wherever they could; and the sun, just dipping below the horizon, spewed a few wimpy orange rays on to the underbelly of the grey and black cotton-wool clouds that clogged the sky.

As the rain continued to fall from the heavens in its almost straight lines, and the surface of the swan's lake seemed to boil and bubble in reaction to the onslaught of the cloud sown, stiff raindrops.

Flashes of lightning were perpetually followed by huge claps of thunder, which was fairly normal for thundery weather as it was the lightning that triggered the loud thunderclaps.

To top it all the wind joined in with the lightning, thunder and rain—not to be outdone - and bashed the lakeside hedges; the ones behind which the swans now sheltered and where, during the summer, they'd cooled off in the shade as happy as feathered bunnies.

"Come on you 'orrible lot it's time we got going," Jonesy started. "It's now 18:20 hours," he continued, over another particularly loud thunderclap, "and time to leave."

After a short pause Jonesy bellowed, "OKAY FLOCK, OFF WE GO." Jonesy swooshed his huge wings and leapt into the air. "Don't dawdle. Just follow me," he commanded.

Honking in excitement each of the swans in the flock took off to follow Jonesy southwards for the winter.

About 10 miles into their journey, with the rain still streaming out of the clouds and the thunder and lightning still doing the thunder and lightning thing, one of Jonesy's larger and older feathers worked its way loose and started a long plunge, through the turbulent air, towards the ground.

The time was now 8:14pm, or 20:14 hours according to the 24 hour clock, and a special time on Hallowe'en; special because, by strange coincidence, 20:14 hours or *twenty fourteen hours*' was an exact anagram of a small part of the ancients' sacred Hallowe'en chant; *Notnefurt-Ou-thyweers*', which roughly translates, into today's English, as, '*Without effort you will yowl when thighs grow under your ears*'.

In the fading brightness arms had sprouted

It is unfortunate but the rest of the actual chant

is lost to history. However, accounts of it and its outcomes were widely written about at the time; and it is in these accounts that other outcomes are suggested, especially if you've been hit by lightning.

The rain lashed the feather. Lightning struck the feather. And anyone who saw the feather as it fell through the sky, in the fading brightness of the lightning flashes, would be sure that somehow arms had sprouted from the chestnut-brown feather's pale shaft—'*the quill bit*', as some brutal feather mangling people called it.

In the turbulent sky an exceptionally large and dark cloud seemed to heave in a deep, deep breath, before lighting up from the inside, and then sneezing out another strike of lightning, which, again, hit the poor wet and miserable looking feather as it hurtled towards the ground.

In most cases this would be viewed as very unlucky, but as these incidents were during the 'special time' on Hallowe'en the worst that happened was that a couple of legs grew out from the shaft close to the feather's base, the end some people might sharpen if they had an inkwell.

Flash.

The feather was hit again; a pair of beady black eyes popped open above its shoulders and looked around rather startled.

Flash.

"Ow," yelped the feather just after it was hit for the fourth time and had gained a mouth.

Flash.

"Oooo," the feather continued, putting newly grown hands into its newly gained pockets.

"Oooo," it said again, slightly more confused this time as the feather discovered it couldn't reach the bottom of the pockets in its skin-tight yellow leggings; the fact they were skin-tight didn't register in the feather's mind as something peculiar or inappropriate for a being of its kind.

After the lightning strikes it had received the feather had changed completely; it was now a strange feather-like being. Down its back swept the chestnut-brown barbs that made up the feather's vanes, the parts of the feather that had, until recently, been the parts that had caught the air when Jonesy had flapped his huge wings.

A third of the way down the feather's shaft, from its tip, was the feather-being's oval head sporting large cheeks, penetrating eyes and, more importantly, a broad smile, though this was to be short lived.

Beneath its neck the feather's shaft expanded into the athletic body-type most track and field competitors hoped to achieve during training—though most would probably prefer not to get there by being struck by lightning multiple times—and this body was clad, head to toe, in a very tight yellow body suit, although each foot was covered by a thigh-length, laced, bright red leather boot.

But being so impressively dressed didn't afford the feather-being any benefit. It rolled and twisted in the air on its journey towards the ground; the rain making it heavy and the wind sending it this way and that. As the feather-being neared the ground it rolled onto its front one final time, and looked through its new eyes at where it was going; and it was not impressed.

Oh no, the feather thought when it saw the gooey, sticky and wet mud, it was about to collide with. The feather-being's broad smile became a tight-lipped straight line.

Chapter 4
Tariq and the Strange Utterances

THWAP

Tariq almost jumped out of his skin, which was quite amazing for him as he had a very thick green and brown flecked shell surrounding it.

What on earth was that noise? Tariq thought, gingerly detaching himself from the ceiling of his hutch.

Tariq was an unfortunate creature; unlike the rest of his kin he was wide-awake. He should have been sound asleep, and be sound asleep for at least the next five months, six if he was going to be lucky, and this was if his friends were to be believed. But this wasn't to be, as Tariq was an insomniac; he just couldn't sleep as tortoises ought to be able to.

Once a year, in April, all of his mates would meet up at the 'Tall Story Tortoise Talkathon' to catch up on old times, have a good laugh at the old Aesop yarn about the hare, and make general chit chat about the dreams they had had over the previous six months.

Tariq wasn't quite sure what a dream was, but he was certain that he would probably like to have one.

Once it had been mentioned, at the Talkathon, that he may have insomnia and this was probably why he didn't dream. But Tariq thought it was just a word his mates had made up just to tease him.

Tariq the tortoise poked his head out of his hutch. *What horrible weather*, he thought. Squinting through the rain and the dark he saw something lying in the mud at the end of his chicken wire pen. It seemed to be attempting to unstick itself from the goo.

Ah! So that's what the noise was, Tariq mused. *But what is it?*

Tariq shut his hutch door and went to his Ottoman chest—the very old, heavy lidded, deep wooden box that he kept some of his special things in.

He opened its lid and pulled out his trusty yellow umbrella, his sunglasses, an old bin liner and a dictionary, then shoved them all but the umbrella into his canvas satchel which he slung over his shoulder. *Now* he was fully prepared, he was ready to go and investigate the unusual noises.

Before leaving his hutch Tariq picked his trusty pea-green deerstalker hat, from his mahogany hat and coat stand, and put it on to protect himself—mainly his head—from the pouring rain.

Tariq went to investigate the unusual noises

He closed his hutch door behind him and edged his way down the wet and slippery wooden ramp that led up to his hutch. Once at the end he carefully and quietly placed his bin liner on the rain-sodden ground. He looked towards the end of his pen, some five metres away, to see if he could see what had made the strange and disturbing noise he'd heard.

The thing that had landed there didn't look like it was going to make any attempt to move towards him; although it was making multiple attempts to sit up rather like a flea would if it had somehow become stuck on its back on the surface, and at the centre, of a very large strawberry jelly.

Jumping on to the bin liner Tariq thrust the top of his up-turned umbrella into the ground and pushed himself forward, punting over the sludgy mud towards the shivering shape at the end of his pen.

As he got closer he dragged the top of his umbrella backwards through the mud to slow himself down.

He didn't like this, didn't like it one bit. Tariq reached into his satchel and removed the sunglasses then placed them on his belt.

The shape had freed itself slightly and was now attempting to sit up.

"Halt! Who sits there?" Tariq called out pretending to be heroic, ever readying his sunglasses; sunglasses were always a useful tool in this type of situation.

"Herm-ave," the shape moaned

The strange shape pondered the question that had come at it out of the dark as if it had just appeared in the air. Then an idea popped into its head. "Hmmmerr," the shape uttered after a very long and silent pause.

Tariq, for the second time this evening, tried to leap out of his skin. He really hadn't expected this thing in the mud to make any kind of noise at all.

Fortunately his shell saved him once more. Tariq was certain that one day his shell would say, "*Oh, go on then*," and just let his skin go, but it wasn't going to be this night.

"Er. What? Pardon?" Tariq didn't have the knack of interrogating shapes of unknown origin, it wasn't anything he'd needed to do before, but he was learning fast.

"herm-ave," the shape moaned, as it attempted to explain its very first idea.

Tariq reached for his satchel and pulled out Colin's Dictionary of Unknown Vocabulary, 'Hermave', Tariq pondered, "Is that with one 'r' or two?"

"hime ave," the shape said more firmly.

"Sorry, you got me there as well. Can't find 'hermave' or 'herrmave' and neither can I find 'hime ave'. Can you mime it?"

With this said the shape struggled, lurched, wobbled, and finally pulled itself up to its entire height of around sixty centimetres: From head to toe the shape dripped goo.

"Whoa!" Tariq said, taken aback, almost leaping from his skin once again.

"If you do that once more," Tariq's shell bemoaned. "I will stay in the hutch for the next five years or until you get so bored you decide to try eating your furniture with marmalade on. I will not suffer these bashings every time your lily-livered head decides to take fright at anything it feels like. OKAY?"

After all the years Tariq had spent on his own, during the winter months wide awake, he'd taken to talking to his shell just to pass the time. Now she had become almost real, someone he could chat to and unfortunately someone who he had lots of disagreements with.

Tremendous, thought Tariq. "Okay!... sorry."

Next the shape, which now looked like a rather large flattened, brown, gloopy banana, started gesturing towards its chest. Following this movement it then vigorously gestured at Tariq. The flat brown gloopy banana shape then spluttered, "Ou r ou?"

Tariq took his up-turned umbrella, stuck it back into the mud, and punted away from the strange banana shape to what he considered a safe distance, all the while making sure that he stayed within his skin.

Tariq didn't exactly like the thought of having

to eat marmalade for the next five years, even if it was on his favourite furniture; he didn't have enough furniture to last five years, or marmalade for that matter.

As the chance arrived he quickly thumbed through Colin's Dictionary of Unknown Vocabulary only to find that, once again, the utterances from the unknown individual were truly unknown unknowns to Colin. Tariq wondered why he had ever borrowed Colin's dictionary in the first place. It was truly useless. He made a mental note to give it back the next time he bumped into Colin.

Looking up from the dictionary he discovered, to his shock and horror, that the gloopy brown shape was now making its way towards him across the wet slurry that formed the end of his pen.

Mentally instructing the head of his liver not to turn into a lily he grabbed the sunglasses from his belt.

Wait 'til you see the whites of its eyes, whites of its eyes, he instructed himself.

"It hasn't got any whites of its eyes," Tariq's shell piped up.

"Well that's just tremendous. Thanks for your help, Shell. Will you now, please, just shut up."

NO WHITES OF EYES, Tariq shouted to himself in his head, *Argh!* he continued. *What do I do now?... I know, I'll wait to see the pinks of its palms.*

"They're red," Tariq's shell stated, more than clearly.

"Right! OKAY! I'll wait 'til I see the reds of its palms. Now just be quiet...RED?"

"It's wearing gloves," Shell replied. Tariq hadn't noticed the gloves in the dark. Everything looked mostly the same colour in the dark.

Tariq stood there, on his bin liner raft, knees quivering; umbrella in one hand and sunglasses in the other.

Reds of its palms, reds of its palms, he told himself again and again.

The globby brown mass was now staggering

towards Tariq, every now and then lurching from one side to the other just catching its balance each time.

Get ready; get ready, any minute now, Tariq thought trying to control the ever increasing urge to propel himself backwards as fast as he could, away from the brown thing-being.

Then it was within range, the distance Tariq had determined to be just right so he could hit the thing-being with his secret weapon sunglasses.

Tariq took aim and threw the sunglasses at the strange shape as if he had been throwing a Frisbee; round and round the sunglasses span, flying through the air towards their intended target.

THWACK, the sunglasses attached themselves

THWACK, the sunglasses attached themselves

just about where the brown shape's eyes ought

to be, if, in fact, it had any. It was too dark to

tell if it had been a direct hit.

The force of the sunglasses spun the gloopy

brown shape around. The shape threw its arms

into the air to steady itself, but to no avail.

It had just a second to wonder why everything, all of a sudden, had gone completely dark before the force of the hit unbalanced it, forcing it to tumble into the sticky mud, back on its back. The shape was now where it had started from.

Tariq made use of the opportunity. Quickly he turned around and used the up-turned umbrella to start punting back up the pen, across the surface of the goo as fast as he could, towards the ramp and the entrance to his hutch.

The greater the distance Tariq managed to put between himself and the gloopy brown thing with red palms the better he felt. Gradually he started to relax.

Only three more metres to go. He made another huge punt and then another. Something was wrong, very wrong, he was slowing down. Tariq attempted a third huge punt, which felt a little too easy for his liking. He looked to where his umbrella was meant to be.

Uh oh! he thought. His hands were empty. Tariq looked back down the pen. In the gloom he could make out, some two metres away, some two metres towards the gloopy brown flat banana like object, a grimy yellow umbrella sticking up out of the mud.

Oh no! I'm marooned, I can't go across the mud without the bin liner because I'll sink and stick and die. Oh no! I'm not going anywhere because the umbrella is stuck. And surely, very soon, that awful gloopy brown flat banana will certainly realise why it's so dark now. And when that happens it will seek me out, track me down and who knows what it'll do then. Oh, oh, oh! Tariq moaned to himself.

He was almost ready to leap out of his skin again, but realising he would still be stuck in the same place he thought better of it.

"Paddle," said Shell.

"What?"

"Just paddle," Shell re-iterated.

"Welllll it's about time too. This is certainly a turn up for the books. My Shell actually saying something useful. Well, I'll be. And just for your information, that was exactly what I was going to do anyway," Tariq said, indignantly.

"Didn't sound like it to me. '*I'll sink and stick and die*'," Shell taunted, quoting Tariq's earlier thoughts.

Ignoring Shell Tariq got down on his stomach, reached over the side of the bin liner and started paddling as fast as he could. He looked back over his shoulder, nothing was moving apart from the rain coming out of the sky, the trees blowing in the wind and his bin liner, which was gradually picking up speed over the mud, moving towards the ramp and his lovely warm hutch. Tariq continued to paddle and then glanced back once more and was worried; the gloopy brown thing had disappeared—it was no longer where it had been.

Tremendous! Tariq thought to himself, not for the first time that day.

Chapter 5
Voices, clips and mud

Dave didn't know what to make of the situation. Everything for him was very new. Even the idea of thinking for himself was new.

Not *ever* having had any thoughts of his own before, the fact that his *very first idea* was to call himself 'Dave', all on his own, was, to say the least, quite exciting and tingly.

Then Dave realised he'd just been speaking! Or at least trying to, though the mud had not made it easy. *SPEAKING!* he thought again. No feather, as far as he could remember, had ever spoken OUT LOUD before! Usually they just thought at each other, with their collective mind—a single mind shared between them all, as they held tight and helped Jonesy thrust the air backward and downward pushing him higher and higher into the sky.

Dave slapped his forehead in an attempt to shake the totally amazing thoughts, in his head, into smaller and easier ones to handle.

Then more amazement washed over him. *I just slapped my forehead*, he thought. His mouth dropped open in a large 'O' shape, and not even the mud that fell into his mouth could make him less surprised. *I just slapped my forehead*, he thought again, but a little louder this time. He'd been able to slap his forehead and this could only mean one thing - he had a HAND! AND it had to be attached to an ARM!

He thought, *If I only had two hands I would slap my forehead twice*. Out of nowhere a force snapped his head back into the mud, twice.

I HAVE TWO HANDS! he thought loudly to himself. Then he thought, *OW!* as his bruised forehead began to sting.

The feather that was once a small part of a community of feathers, called the *Jonesy Featherdom*, began to know that his very experience of featherdom was changing beyond anything he'd ever imagined, not that he had ever imagined anything before his change because it had been the Jonesy Featherdom that had been doing the imagining. The thousands of voices that used to echo through his head had become nothing more than a distant whisper.

The ability to move independently from the rest of the crowd was freeing, but at the same time felt like a loss as well—he had no one to talk to, no one with whom he could discuss the effects of rain whilst flying, no one he could approach about the issues of wax—but, unlike being with the rest of the featherdom, he had the option to decide for himself who he could talk to, who he would talk to, who he would shake HANDS with—as he thought about the idea of 'hands' he smiled to himself—he, Dave, had hands; and hands of such a nature they were able to slap his forehead. He had changed, in fact, he had been changed.

Whether it had been the Thunder Gods' electrical spite that had soaked the chestnut brown feather with life and vigour or some other supernatural being, Dave was here and 'Seventh of Two Hundred and Eighteen Thousand and Twelve', as he'd been known in the Jonesy Featherdom, had moved on.

Although what had happened had happened Dave was aware that this was the first time he'd been away from his fellow feathers, and somehow he'd ended up with a stinging clip around the face, a total blackout and his mouth filled with wet and gooey mud.

He was used to being covered with dry mud during the summer, whilst taking a bath with the rest of Jonesy's featherdom, but had never had to have a clip around the face to do that. *A FACE!* he thought to himself, and grinned.

Dave then continued to ponder his predicament. *Must be the rain*, he thought. The mud was not strictly unpleasant, but it did make speaking rather difficult; and moving, well, that was almost an impossibility.

In the dismal winter weather, in the dark, he hadn't quite been able to make out the shape that had been pushing sounds at him.

Apart from the clip around the face, his mouth being filled with mud, and the fact that he was stuck in the mud on his back, he was certain the shape, which had been yelling at him, was essentially friendly. Dave lifted himself onto his elbows. *ELBOWS!* he thought, and smiled.

However, he continued to think, *that's the last time I judge a book by its cover, especially when I can't see it in the dark. So from now on I can judge a book by its cover only when I can actually see it, before I make any judgement.*

Happy with this reasoning, Dave flopped back into the goo to consider what he was going to do next.

Chapter 6
Logical?

"Yesssss, huzzar, most spondicious," Tariq said aloud as his dustbin liner raft glided the last few metres across the goo of his pen to the ramp, which led up to his soaking wet, wooden hutch.

The strange gloopy-being had scared him, a bit, but he'd won and now he was back at the bottom of the ramp, and very nearly back in his pleasantly warm hutch; and now he was feeling, sort of, okay.

Tariq got off his stomach and stood on the

dustbin liner raft ready to step onto the ramp up to his front door.

For a moment he thought that, by some miracle, his hutch was growing taller—then another, much worse, thought occurred to him; the rain had rained so hard and had made him so wet he'd actually started to shrink. *Oh no!* he thought. He looked at his hand and shook the mud from it. He needed to make sure he wasn't shrinking. How would he pour himself a cup of tea if his tea pot was too big for him to pick it up?

He checked his hands very carefully. *Nope*, he thought, very relieved. *Looks the same size to me*. It was then he noticed both his feet had sunk up to their ankles. The plastic bin liner was unable to support all his weight through his two small feet. The goo continued to suck the bin liner raft down into the ground with gravity's help.

Oh no! I'm sinking, Tariq thought. *Quick!* he told himself. As the thought left his mind he jumped onto the ramp, nearly slipping, his arms wind-milling to regain his balance. After a few scary seconds Tariq managed to steady himself and ran up the ramp into his hutch as fast as he could. Heart a pounding he slammed his hutch door shut and bolted it.

Tremendous, he thought.

"Chicken!" Tariq's shell exclaimed for all the

world to hear.

"IIII'mmmm soooo glad you're back to your old self, Shell. I wouldn't have known what to do if you hadn't been," Tariq said sarcastically.

Tariq knew that the next things he did in his present predicament were going to be very important. Something had landed in his pen, without permission, and without any shape, and Tariq was going to have to deal with it.

Being a gifted insomniac tortoise, as his friends always called him, (actually they just called him insomniac, he'd decided to add the gifted bit), meant that he was entitled to have his own way to sort out the problems he had to face every now and then.

It was time to make sense of everything that had happened since the big *thwap*, and the moments since he'd stuck his head out of his hutch.

He got out his mental notebook and read through the points he'd made earlier.

1. *Big* thwap,

2. *Wet head*

3. *Gooey mud*

4. *Peculiar gloopy thing*

5. *Frisbee sunglasses*

Tariq was certain he'd left something out. If only he could just grasp that part, then, perhaps, he could make sense of the whole situation.

He racked his brains struggling to think of the missing point, the part that would reveal all the hidden mysteries that were yet to be revealed.

Only one more thing, he thought to himself. *Just one thing*, he continued to think. *What is it? What is it?* Then the thought struck him. *YES! I've got it, 5B—heroic return.*

Now he had all the information in place it was time to work out what it meant.

If 1 led to 2 and 2 indicated 3, then 3 meant there was 1, which also meant there was 4, and as there was 4 then there must be 5. And 5B, of course. "Tremendous!" Tariq exclaimed to himself. "I've figured it out."

"Great," said Shell. Being Shell she was able

to hear everything Tariq thought, much to his disappointment—although sometimes it was helpful not having to repeat what he'd thought if he'd needed her opinion ever. This time he didn't but she continued anyway. "So you've worked out that you've read all your notes, the ones you made based on your experiences. *FANTASTIC!*"

"Shell, you just don't understand the meaning of this. There's something out there that's trying to hide. And this means it doesn't want to be seen. And this fact alone tells me it won't be bothering me ever again."

"And?" snapped Shell.

"'*And?*'", Tariq repeated. "It's simple; I can

forget about it. This evening's events are over. I can make myself a nice cup of tea from a tea pot that is a *normal* size and sit back on the sofa whilst I watch some of my 'Marvelman the Fish' DVDs."

"Well," Shell started hesitantly, "I'm certainly happy you've made that clear to me now. NOT!"

Chapter 7
Mud and Presents

Dave stood up once again and tried to shake off all the dirt he'd accumulated during his journey to the ground, but more importantly the goo he'd been covered in when he'd hit the sloppy mud.

He reached for his eyes and removed the strange object that had become wedged on his face, after his meeting with the peculiar mud gliding individual—not that it had been a meeting, as such, because the distance between him and the odd, capped, yelling thing had been the same as him trying to chat to feathers on a bird that wasn't Jonesy.

He examined the object. It was marked with two words separated by a hyphen; *Ray-Ban*. Dave was impressed even though he didn't understand the value of the marking, the object just looked great. He tried them on again and in the dark, rain filled evening light, everything disappeared once more. Dave pulled them off. *Interesting*, he thought. *Must be a greeting present. Not sure why I should have one,* he continued to think, *but obviously they want to meet me. And why not?* he decided.

As he'd lain in the goo at the end of the pen,

in his new body, Dave had wondered about things and he'd certainly had never assumed that he'd be anything more than a friend to anyone he met. It was obvious that his current situation was a little bit more complicated to comprehend than he'd thought it would be.

For a start, why would anyone want to give him a present so forcefully? Could it be, perhaps, they just wanted to be *real* close friends? These thoughts didn't fit with the fact that the '*real close friend*' had disappeared back up the pen, across the muddy goo and into the hutch so fast, after giving him the 'Ray-Ban' present, that it seemed the '*real close friend*' didn't want to be friends.

Dave shook his head at the thought—it was stupid. More likely the '*real close friend*' wanted to be friends so much that they'd raced back to their home so they could tidy up and make it right, ready for Dave's visit.

Whatever, Dave continued thinking. *Perhaps they're just a little bit shy*.

Somehow, although he didn't know how, he was aware that everyone had their own way of making friends. But he still had to admit to himself that this way had been a little bit more extreme than most!

Dave went on to shake off the extra wet dirt by performing the secret wet dirt removal dance. Before he started he had a quick look around. It was essential there were no onlookers as this was the 'sacred wet dirt removal' dance that was only to be known by his kind—no one could ever find out.

It was also the way every bird cleaned themselves—the wet dirt sticking to unwanted feather pests and taking them from the feathers during the course of the special dance the feathers performed.

After a few side steps, a back bend and a little shimmy he was clear of the worst of the wet dirt. Now it was time to make his way to the hutch, the hutch of the 'real' friend, and introduce himself.

Dave stomped his way up the pen not

bothering about the mud. He was light enough and more than capable of tackling this level of stickiness, or so he assumed.

Abruptly he came to a halt. He was now concerned. He was not able to shift his legs in any direction; he was now up to his waist in the goo.

It was obvious that without any help he was going nowhere. He tried to shift his legs once more only to find, to his dismay, that he just sunk further into the mud.

Dave looked around in desperation and caught a glimpse of a yellow stick like object protruding from the mud. Not really a stick but more of an umbrella, but Dave was not aware of such things.

There's no way I'm going to become stuck, he thought to himself, even though he was already waist deep in the mud. His only chance was the strange yellow stick, but this was not quite in his reach.

Somehow Dave knew that if he moved too vigorously the mud would take him and if he didn't the mud would still take him anyway. He made one final effort, thrusting one of his new arms towards the yellow stick to grab it in one of his new red-gloved hands.

The goo sucked at his body, his arm shook with the effort as he strained and stretched as he attempted to grab the stick.

Is this it? Is this to be my end? he thought. Suddenly the howling wind grew in intensity and the yellow stick wobbled further from his reach.

"Ohh nooo," Dave yelled in frustration. Then, "Oww that hurt."

A branch from a nearby tree had blown free in the wind and cracked him over the head on its journey across the muddied garden. His predicament had got worse. The bash on the bonce had hammered him further into the gooey mud. Dave was now up to his chest. The wind carried on blowing without a care.

HOWL, WHOOSH, WHOOSH, the wind continued, CRACK!

"Ow, ow — Ow, ow," went Dave.

Yet another branch had been blown free and cracked him across his head. This time the branch had ended up in the mud next to him. He was about to pick it out of the goo and break it into little bits, just out of annoyance, when a thought struck him.

"Ow," he said again. He'd been struck with enough things already this evening, his head not having yet recovered from the branches, and being struck by this thought had just been the icing on the cake.

As it turned out this was a good 'Ow'. He picked up the branch and holding it level to the ground he moved it around to hook the yellow stick-thing's shaft, then pulled it towards him.

Grabbing the stick he pulled himself slowly from the mud and, after some effort, eventually got himself and his legs free. In that instant he leapt on to the yellow stick circling his arms and legs around it.

This is perfect, he thought.

Bending his knees and then stretching them again he managed to make the yellow stick move as if it was a pogo.

"Good." He felt the mud give way slightly. Holding the shaft of the yellow stick more firmly, to secure his position, he suddenly became unbalanced. His feet were thrown out from under him without any obvious reason. It was fortunate he'd managed to keep a firm grip on the yellow stick's shaft.

Whootompsch, went the yellow stick.

"Whooaah," went Dave.

The stick suddenly transformed itself; the bottom of the shaft opened up into a coracle like object. Dave was now clear of the gooey mud and was standing in an up turned open yellow hemisphere. It was a bit like a ping pong ball that had been cut in half, about the size of the top of an upturned umbrella.

What an amazing piece of luck, Dave thought as he stared at the yellow material that was now between himself and the mud.

Bending his knees, once again, and leaping upward as he held on to the shaft, Dave managed to pogo the coracle towards the ramp of the hutch.

He was determined to get to the ramp and off the mud at the very least. With each jump he made he got nearer the ramp, and his chance to get away from the sticky muddy goo increased with each leap he made.

Chapter 8
Tea Noises

After bolting the door to his hutch behind him and having a '*little*' discussion with Shell, Tariq needed a cup of tea, something that would calm his nerves.

He lifted his old-fashioned conical, dark metallic blue kettle by its black Bakelite handle and put it under the tap to fill it with water. Once filled he placed it on one of the gas rings on his white enamelled oven.

Whilst he waited for the steam in the kettle

to build up enough to whistle the kettle's whistle he thought about the evening he'd had and shook his head. It had been a very troublesome and traumatic evening, but he could forget it— he'd won, hadn't he?—he insisted to himself.

He was happy that the whole episode of the really peculiar weather and the strange landing of the banana-like thing had finished without further ado; but something still felt wrong, something was not quite correct.

As soon as the peep of the kettle's whistle sounded, telling him it had boiled, he turned the gas off and took the kettle from the oven's burner, then poured the hot water into his lilac teapot; he smiled as he looked upon its amusing decorations of little white rabbits crossing a finish line ahead of a tortoise. Tariq loved how the artist had captured the irony—little did any other animal species know what tortoises could really do.

He sat down at his wooden kitchen table. He'd made its top from a few pale-green painted planks, then propped them up by adding four square white painted legs. He stirred the teapot.

Ssschlop, ftumch!

Tariq looked around and wondered where the strange noise had come from. He lifted the lid from his decorated teapot and looked inside, there were a few tea bags floating around—he stirred them, peered over the rim of the pot once again and then put his ear to its top. Nothing! The tea bags didn't make a sound. Tariq was now certain that the strange noise hadn't come from his teapot.

He sat back down, stirred the teapot once more, replaced its lid, and lifted it to pour some tea into his pale green china tea cup.

After the traumas of the day Tariq felt happy. He looked around the inside of his hutch and thought '*home*'. He was secure here and could fulfil his obligations, the things he needed to do, as one of tortoise-kind, with ease and attentiveness.

He added milk to his tea. Then stirred the tea until the dark mahogany-brown liquid became a milky light-brown.

Tariq was looking forward to this refreshing drink, because he'd earned it, after he'd seen off the strange thing from the outside.

He lifted the cup to his mouth, his thumb and forefinger holding the cup's handle, and tipped it so he could taste its refreshing flavour.

But before he could finish, before a single drop could enter his mouth, the strange noise drifted into his ears once more.

Ssschlop, ftumch

Tariq slowly placed the tea cup back onto its saucer, his nerves ajar. *Oh no*, he thought. He knew now where the noise had come from—it was outside, outside of his hutch, somewhere from the depths of the dark and dreary night.

Ssschlop, ftumch, the noise went again.

Tariq recalled his mental notes, especially 5B, and decided it would be better to take no notice of the strange '*Ssschlop ftumch*' noise. It was probably nothing; the noise had probably been nothing more than the way a tea bag had circulated around his teapot as he'd stirred it.

Tariq, at last, took a drink of his tea, but with each gulp, gulp, that Tariq made as his tea went down, *Ssschlop, ftumch, Ssschlop, ftumch,* could be heard.

Tariq finished his tea and listened.

Ssschlop, ftumch, Ssschlop, ftumch, the noise continued.

He started to shake in his shell. He was waiting for Shell to berate him, but for some reason she remained silent; it became clear that, his Shell, had left him alone when he most needed her.

As Tariq listened it became clear that the noise was not due to some kind of peculiar tea bag movement, nor was it to do with the usual functions of his stomach.

Tariq finished the rest of his tea and decided he'd be better off if he got into his special quilt— the one he'd folded in half and added a zip to— so he could sleep through the awful night's weather without being disturbed.

He zipped the quilt up to his neck and

listened carefully—he couldn't help it—every time he thought there was something in the dark his ears decided to listen harder, just so they could hear the sounds that weren't meant to be heard.

Tariq turned his hutch's lights off. He been told the best way to fall asleep was to have the lights off and let his brain turn off. He turned the lights off. Then he groaned. He was an insomniac, a gifted one at that, but that meant one thing; no matter how hard he tried he would never get to sleep.

He poked an ear out of the top of his special quilt and listened.

Ssschlop, ftumch. Ssschlop, ftumch.

The noise continued. Tariq shook his head in misery. *What on earth could it be?* he wondered. It wasn't a normal sound by anyone's measure.

For Tariq it was definitely time to zip up the quilt, across the top, so he became completely sealed in, so he could avoid any further need to investigate the strange noises echoing from outside of his hutch.

Although I've had some tea, Tariq pondered to himself, *this doesn't seem to be the end of this peculiar evening... Tremendous!*

Tariq sighed a huge miserable sigh and started to shake in his quilt cocoon, worried about what was going to happen next.

One thing was for sure, he was certain his

specially designed quilt, the one he'd designed, would protect him from the next thing to come.

* * *

Shell had kept quiet for a reason, she knew how worried Tariq was and didn't want to make him worse—there was shaking and shaking and she preferred not to be shaken unnecessarily—but she knew that no matter how much confidence he had in his quilt, he was *too* confident in the powers his zipped quilt possessed. And, in fact, it really wouldn't help him at all.

Chapter 9
Knock, knock, knocking

With his last leap the upturned umbrella made its final '*ssschlop, ftumch,*' noise as it lifted from the muddy goo of the pen and then sploshed back down. The yellow coracle had finally arrived at its destination. Dave stepped from the wobbly goo-floater onto the bottom of the hutch's wooden ramp.

Phew! Dave thought to himself. It had taken a lot of effort to pogo the coracle across the goo of the pen to the safety of the hutch.

To make sure the yellow coracle wouldn't blow away in the stormy conditions he found some rope, tied it to the ramp's balustrade, and then attached it to the handle of the coracle.

Once finished he winked at his trusty mud transport. "Thank you, my trusty coracle," he said. "You have served me well and you will be rewarded."

Dave didn't have any idea how he could reward the upturned umbrella as he knew the umbrella was, in fact, inanimate and unable to understand or comprehend anything he said. And even if it did, what would an upturned umbrella actually want?—Dave had no idea, and as he had more important things to consider he left the idea where it was.

However, he'd said it all the same, and winked, because he could, because he was enjoying his new ability to talk, and shut one eye whilst keeping the other open.

Dave smiled to himself. Life was good. He stomped up the ramp with an excitement he was finding difficult to contain. He knew, in a few moments, he would be meeting his *real friend,* real soon.

Dave lifted his hand and gazed at his amazing red gloves; it was the first time he'd seen them properly; the light from the hutch's window allowing him to seem them properly for the first time. Dave shook his head in admiration. *How awesome are those hand covering things?* he thought, and then nodded to himself in agreement.

He knocked on the entrance to Tariq's hutch. *Knock, knock, knock.*

Tariq poked his head out of his quilt and looked towards his front door. After a short pause it seemed to Dave that perhaps his new friend hadn't quite heard his knocking—possibly due to the awful weather, he considered. So Dave tried again.

Knock, knock, knock.

Tariq saw the door shake with the intensity of the knocking. "Oh no," he sighed utterly disheartened.

Dave stroked his chin with a gloved hand. *A CHIN!* Dave thought to himself—he hadn't realised he'd had one until then. He smiled. *Hmm*, he thought. He decided to try again.

Knock, knock, knock.

Tariq sealed himself into his quilt of invisibility. Not that the quilt was invisible itself, nor that he would actually become invisible. But Tariq was sure that if he couldn't see *it*, whatever *it* was knocking at the door, then *it* couldn't see him. Which was true as long as *it* remained outside his hutch, knocking at his door.

Tariq was pleased he'd planned for this so long ago. The steps he'd taken was completely in line with *the plan, his plan.* The idea to be disguised as a quilt, some kind of ordinary furniture or accessory, something that wouldn't be noticed, had struck him after a visit from his friends a few years ago, when they'd popped in for a cup of tea on their way to the Tall Story Tortoise Talkathon.

His friends had pointed out, "That bed is so boring that even if you lay there waiting for the teaspoon of death to take you away, it still wouldn't be able to find you."

The notion had occurred to him whilst pondering his fellow tortoises' views about how his bed was styled.

He knew his bed would wrap around his

body. And if he was camouflaged as a quilt it was a certainty that he would not be discovered. In this way, if and when, any knocking thing decided to knock, and then find some way to enter his hutch he couldn't be noticed, let alone found.

In fact, he knew he'd be totally invisible because his quilt of camouflage would make him non-existent; and when the thing entered it would take a quick glance around his hutch and say *'Oh! There's nothing here,'* then leave utterly bored stiff.

Chapter 10
After Tea, Bed?

Dave knocked at the door for a fourth time. And, again, nothing happened.

How am I going to get out of this awful weather? Dave wondered. *Please let this door open—I'm officially fed up with the weather out here. It's horrible.*

Dave examined the door and noticed that there was a bolt keeping it closed. A surprised frown crossed his brow. Should he believe what he was seeing?

If I slide this bolt sideways then, Dave started to think, *potentially, I would be able to get in.*

Dave slid the bolt sideways and pulled the hutch's door open. He staggered into the hutch battling another large gust of wind and quickly closed the door behind him, shutting out the night's storm.

As he looked around the wooden walled interior he knew instantly where to get some tea.

This is strange, he thought. *Where is that nice person who showed me such kindness, by giving me some dark eye-wear for this awful black and wet evening?*

Dave continued to look around the room. He saw the tea pot, he saw the larder, and he saw the sleeping area. Nothing in his observation said to him that the hutch actually had a living occupant.

Dave was now very curious and a few questions had instantly come to mind. Who or what had given him, albeit in a very forceful manner, a decent pair of sun glasses? Who or what had left a yellow coracle for him to get across the mud? And who or what had prepared the tea and laid it out on a pale green table, ready for him to have a drink? Dave decided to ignore these questions and just go for the tea. He was in particular need of some refreshment.

He needed a pick-me-up. The journey across the sloppy mud of the pen he'd landed in, had been hard and exhausting. Dave poured out the tea and sat down on the nearest chair.

It was clear to him that he had a few important things to think about. Sitting down and drinking tea was one way to start to understand all that had happened. As he supped his tea he mulled over what had gone on.

Dave looked around the room again. One thing was for sure, the bed, where he would like to lay down, and rest, did not seem to be a particularly comfortable place to rest.

Looking at it, the bed struck him as very lumpy. There was a duvet, laid out across the bed, which rose, towards its centre, to a height that was definitely not normal—the mound looking like some kind of hutch-sized, small hill.

Forgetting the lump in the duvet's middle, the duvet itself was peculiar as well. It had a zip that had been very badly stitched to its side and around its top.

There was no real reason for him to be concerned about this apart from the fact that if he were to use this bed for the purposes of sleep, the lump had to go. He supped his tea again and studied the bed, carefully.

Another question raised itself in his mind, *Why does this bed seem to be shaking?*

As Dave looked at the bed he could see that

the covers could not be described as tranquil, furthermore, they could not even be seen as remotely steady. Dave was going off the idea of tucking down and sleeping on the bed.

I mean, Dave thought. *Who would want to sleep on a shaking bed*? As the thought occurred to him it seemed, truly, that a shaking bed couldn't be normal, and something else was definitely going on.

He was not only in a hutch, but he was in a hutch that included the, all but impossible, shaking bed as well! Now he had to choose; a seat, or a vibrating bed to sleep on.

Dave decided that in ordinary circumstances, the ones that he'd heard about, a shaking bed could be quite intriguing; however, in this case, he was absolutely sure there was something to be discovered, a mystery that needed to be revealed.

Because of the fact he'd had an extremely complicated evening so far, he decided he would finish his tea first, and then attempt to understand the shaking bed. Dave gulped down his tea.

Feeling refreshed he decided to seek out the best place to sleep. There was really no other place to sleep, apart from the lumpy bed; a lumpy and quivering bed at that. Considering all the options, i.e. bed or not bed, he decided to leap on to the quivering mass to determine where the buttons of the control unit were, so that he could turn the quivering off.

"Aarrgrahaa," yelped the bed.

"Aarrgrahaa," Dave responded.

"Yeowl," the bed carried on. Dave leapt off the bed and looked at it critically. The bed continued to shake and shiver.

Dave frowned. *Why is it, whenever I try to do something normal, it just doesn't work out right?* he thought.

"Go away," said the bed. "You're not invited... you're not allowed in here."

Dave did a double take and looked at the bed again. "Who are you?...," Dave started.

"Go away," the bed re-stated firmly.

"No," Dave said even more firmly. "You are a bed and it is your purpose to provide adequate comfort for the provision of sleep, for those of us who would like the choice of sleeping or not, as the case may be."

"Okay. That may be so," the bed continued. "But, I am not a bed... I am a living being, one which deserves the space that I have claimed for myself—the interior of my hutch—as it is my due!"

Understanding exactly what the bed meant, Dave disagreed. "So, essentially, you, as a duvet or bed, believe you're the only one entitled to the horizontal position you have claimed for yourself, and henceforth there shall not be any other that wouldst partake of this positioning other than another duvet?"

"No," said the bed.

Dave frowned. "No?" he queried.

"No. It is entirely possible that a quilt or duvet or bed, as you may have it, may merely be a quilt or a duvet or a bed, and that the voice of the bed maybe some other voice of a being not yet perceived at this moment!". Tariq responded. He was now wondering whether he could come out on top of this conversation.

Dave considered what had been said. "Okay—Show yourself," he demanded.

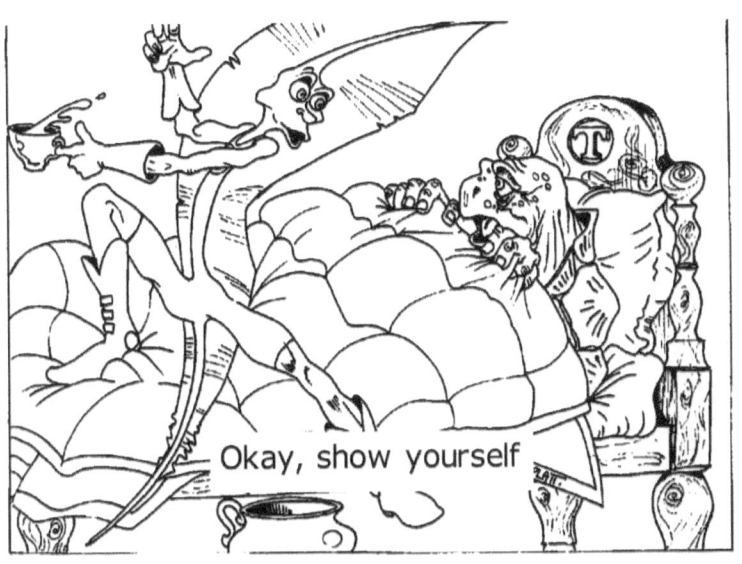

Okay, show yourself

Tariq thought about the proposition. He knew that if this situation was not resolved, now, further consequences were, more likely than not, to be expected. Being the brave and heroic person Tariq was, he unzipped his quilt-duvet-sleeping bag and threw off the cover.

"Aarrgrahaa," screamed Shell at the top of

her voice trying not to smirk as she did so.

Tariq collapsed on the floor at Dave's feet, shocked into a dead faint.

Dave was a little surprised.

Chapter 11
Friends? Not Quite.

Now that the lump had revealed itself to be more tortoise than actual lump, and had removed itself from the bed in the process, Dave took his chance.

He stepped over the unconscious body of the tortoise and leapt onto the bed. Then tested it. Lying on his back Dave bounced his bum up and down on the mattress. *A BUM!* he thought and smiled, liking the idea he had a posterior.

This is very comfy, he thought, and was

about to consider the fact he may get some rest after all when, without warning, he fell asleep.

For both Dave and Tariq the evening had been very traumatic and difficult for various reasons; but both were very glad to be out of the weather.

After a few hours of filling the hutch with snores Tariq's eyes slammed open. He looked around whilst his brain tried to figure out what had gone on, and where it had been. Tariq looked at his bed, and then it all came back to him.

"Who are you?" Tariq demanded.

For a moment Dave thought that some big hand had grabbed him from the sky and had started pulling him down towards a sea of brown muddiness. Then he opened his eyes and shook his head shaking the remains of the dream from it. "What?" he asked, slightly confused and befuddled.

"I said: Who are you?" Tariq demanded once again.

"Dave," Dave said, now fully awake. "And I could ask you the very same question."

"Okay," Tariq replied. "Let me put it this way." Tariq couldn't believe how brave he sounded, but when someone steals your bed, according to tortoise-kind law, because beds are very important to tortoises—even if they can't sleep during the autumn and winter—a tortoise has to do something.

"You have," Tariq started, "forced your way into my house and now you're sitting here, in my bed, telling me that you are Dave.

"Because of this, I suppose, I should be telling you that I am Tariq, Tariq of the Insomniacs—actually, Tariq, the Gifted, of the Insomniacs. And in this light what is your full title?"

"Forced my way in did I?" Dave was astonished by the accusation. "There's a bolt on the outside. On the door, in fact," Dave replied. "I slid it sideways and the door opened."

"Yes. But the outside bolt is only for my use, just in case I lock myself out! And what about the sign?"

"What sign?"

"The sign on the bolt that says, 'For Tariq's Use Only'."

"There is no sign."

Tariq thought about this and then remembered that his sign was still on the bench in his workshop waiting to be re-painted. "And, as I said before, what is your full title?" Tariq pushed on, dismissing the matter of the sign.

"I'm Dave," and thinking quickly to himself he added, "I am Dave, seventh of two hundred and eighteen thousand, three hundred and ninety four." Dave suspected this number was a pretty good guess at how many others of his kind were in the Jonesy featherdom, before he'd been blown free. "But most call me Dave for short."

Dave was not a presupposing individual nor wanted to be. In reality Dave didn't have any title but just wanted Tariq, the Gifted of the Insomniacs, to feel comfortable, and if titles were the way then so be it.

The answer Dave had given Tariq wasn't the one he'd been after, but considering what had been said, Tariq decided it would do.

"Thanks for letting me in," Dave added.

Tariq's chin hit the ground. "Letting you in?— Well, Mr Dave Foreshort, I don't think I had any choice did I?"

"Yes and no," said Dave

"Yes and no?" Tariq repeated. "Did I really have a choice?"

"Yes," Dave finished.

"And how is that then?" Tariq said, all the more put out.

"You provided me with the things I needed to get across the goo, and in doing so you gave me the direction! Without planting the yellow coracle I would not have been able to make my way to this fine hutch."

Tariq went over the last half an hour in his mind to make sure that Dave's statement actually fitted with the evening's events. Apart from the coracle everything seemed to fit.

Coracle! Tariq thought to himself. *Coracle*! Tariq thought again. After a few more seconds he understood; *Oh—the umbrella! Now I get it.* Tariq could see that an upside down umbrella could look very much like a coracle.

Yes it was true that Tariq had left the umbrella, yes it was true that Tariq had left his hutch to venture out to see what was going on, and yes it was true that in returning to the hutch he had turned the lights on so he could make a cup of tea, and it was also true that he hadn't put up the sign stating that the outside bolt was only for his own use in case of an emergency. All in all everything Dave was saying was true.

"As you can probably understand," Dave

started, "I mean you no harm, and I expect that you mean me no harm. Especially as you deemed it necessary to give me some Ray-Ban eye-coverings as a present."

Tariq did not know what to make of this. He had never meant anyone any harm ever in his entire lifetime nor did he want to, unless he was defending that, which he believed, was right in the presence of wrongdoing. This was not a wrongdoing situation. Probably not a situation that required defending, but how could he have known this without being informed of it in the first place?

Being of the generous type Tariq said, "Okay. I understand that you have had a particularly hard time this evening, and may well need rest. So I will allow you to stay here until you have recovered from your trauma."

"Thank you. Thank you ever so much, Tariq. I will never forget your kindness, ever," Dave replied.

"Right. It's still the night, the weather is rubbish. You can stay until morning. After that you will have to find your own place. Okay?"

"Many thanks be bestowed upon you, Tariq," Dave offered.

"You feeble minded wally," Shell added.

"What?" asked Dave.

"Nothing," said Tariq. "That was just the wind outside. Ignore her—I mean—it."

Tariq quickly changed the subject not wanting to be drawn into a discussion about Shell; especially to someone he didn't know.

"There is another quilt in the cupboard over there if you need one," Tariq continued, pointing towards the stained oak dresser at the back of his hutch. "But once it is morning I would prefer that you left."

"No probs there, Tariq. It's not my purpose to frequent one place permanently: For I am the helper of all needful things and to do this I must travel."

What an uptight arrogant fool this Dave is, Tariq thought. *And what is it with those gloves and boots? And especially that yellow "D" in a circle on his chest*, he continued thinking, as he eyed Dave's scarlet hand and footwear and yellow bodysuit.

Dave retrieved the spare quilt from the cupboard and pulled it across himself as he settled on Tariq's sofa. Tariq sat down on his bed, pulled his sleeping-bag/quilt around him and then laid down ready for the evening's thoughts, because, being insomniac, he wouldn't be sleeping.

Chapter 12
Strangers Separate

Morning light poured in through Tariq's kitchen window, which overlooked his pen; it glinted off the edges of his white ceramic sink. The morning had truly arrived and it was nice, completely opposite to the previous evening's awfulness.

Dave became aware of the dawn's light, because its brightness was, sort of, lazy and had decided to shine through his closed eyelids.

Still breathing as if he was asleep he opened

his eyes just a crack, then looked around, checking where he was and what was around him.

When he was satisfied there was no danger he opened his eyes fully; he could be seen to be alive, should anyone or anything be watching.

Dave slung one arm over the back of the sofa he'd been using as a bed and lifted himself up. Nothing had changed from the night before, except that his host was no longer on *his* bed or in the quilt / duvet / sleeping bag.

It occurred to Dave that his host, Tariq, couldn't have gone far—there'd been no noise of a front hutch door closing, no noise of someone using a window to leave, and no noise of a person attempting to climb up the oven's chimney to get out of the place. All in all, Dave assumed, no one had left the building.

So, Dave, with nothing else left to do, decided to call out, it being the only option left. "Tariq," he called, "once more I must thank you for the consideration you have shown me. May it be given back to you five-fold—at least."

Dave heard a sound that was almost in the hutch, but at the same time didn't quite sound like it was in the hutch. *Was that something being dropped*, he thought. Dave listened carefully.

"hmmmDon?"

Dave frowned. Although not sure, he was

fairly certain someone had asked him, 'hmmmDon'. He'd never heard this word before. It didn't make any sense to him.

Dave got up from the sofa, and using his ears, he tried to locate the source of the sounds.

EARS! Dave thought, and laughed to himself. Ears were great fun to have, especially if you'd never had them before.

He wandered past the sink and the cooker and made his way to the back of the hutch, past a huge wooden book case.

Dave tried again. "Tariq," he called, "once more I must thank you for the consideration you've shown me. May it be given back to you five-fold—at least."

"Pardon?" Tariq yelled again up the stairs that led from his workshop to his hutch proper. The tortoise's muffled voice drifted out from behind the thick, dark brown rug which hung on the back wall of the hutch.

Dave snooped about a bit more; he looked left and right, up and down, making every attempt to find the source of Tariq's voice. He stopped at a rug hanging on the back wall and repeated his question, "I said...," Dave started, "where are you?" There was no response just a noise.

Domp, domp, domp, domp, domp. The dull thudding sound sounded. It was the sort of noise a tortoise might make travelling at a surprisingly fast pace up some old wooden stairs from a cellar.

"Here," Tariq said, as he poked his head out from behind the old rug curtain. "What did you say?"

"I said, thank you for your consideration, may you get it back five-fold, and I'm leaving."

"Okay, Dave. Perhaps we'll meet again, I don't know where and I don't know when, but I'm sure we'll meet again some sunny day, or perhaps, even, a rainy one. Who knows?"

"Thanks for everything, Tariq; you've been a good person to me. Bye."

Before Dave turned to leave Tariq spoke up. "Wait a moment. I have something that should help." Tariq walked over to his book case and pulled a volume from its shelves. "Have this," Tariq offered.

Dave was stunned. "Why, thank you, Tariq," he replied as he took the offered book and placed the large tome into one of his deep pockets.

With the offer made, and accepted, Dave turned about and made his way to the front door of Tariq's hutch. He pulled it open and made his way outside, making sure to close and bolt its door behind him.

Well, Dave considered, *what a nice person*. Dave strolled down the ramp to Tariq's home and looked for the exit of Tariq's pen. Dave nodded to himself as he spotted the pen's exit then made for it to make his way out.

Fortunately most of the ground's moisture had evaporated and the previous night's struggle was not to be experienced again.

Dave swung open the pen's gate and left the home of Tariq the tortoise, the gifted one, if he were to be believed. *Today is another day*, Dave thought.

Well, Tariq thought as he gazed out of his kitchen window watching the feather-like figure leave. *What a strange person.*

Chapter 13
Nobody Ignores Dave

As Dave walked away from Tariq's hutch and pen he wondered where, exactly, he would now go.

He stood at the rear of Tariq's home and gazed upon a huge house, whose grounds Tariq's hutch seemed to belong to. Dave shook his head.

The house's two first floor windows twinkled in the winter's early morning sunlight, as the bare branches of the trees' tops, which surrounded the house, were pushed lazily back and forth by a light breeze; intermittently blocking and unblocking the morning sun's golden rays. The house's ground level glass door and single window remained dull, the sun unable to break through the tree line at this hour of the morning.

Dave shook his head again. He was amazed. He'd never realised how big houses were, close up—he'd only ever been aware of them as Jonesy flew high in the sky, swooping this way and that, way up in the sky. At that time they'd looked really small; almost toy-like.

His thoughts were interrupted by a strange noise, a sort of on–off low purring sound. It came from the other side of the strangely huge house. Dave being Dave decided to investigate.

He strode across the last bit of the garden's grass and walked down a dimly lit alleyway which separated a wooden fence from the extremely tall wall of the side of the house. The wall wasn't painted like the back of the house—bright white—it was just covered in a dull sandy-grey material with a lot of small stones dotted in it.

Dave wondered how long it had taken the person to push each of the small, shiny pebbles into the dull sand. Then he wondered how the sand had been stuck to the side of the house.

Again he shook his head—everything was so

much more interesting, but more puzzling, in close up.

Another purring sound distracted him from his thoughts and Dave continued along the alleyway to the front of the house. As he stepped from the passage Dave caught a glimpse of a shiny yellow box whizzing by. It followed a row of white dashes that had been marked along the middle of a dark path which tracked past the front of the house.

The dark path (with the dotted lines) had two parallel runs of grass, each included trees, at either of its sides, and between the grass verge and the houses was another path made from squares, some whole and some cracked.

Dave checked his watch. *Great,* he thought, as he discovered he did not possess one. Life was certainly tough as an independent feather, one of his own means.

He plonked down on a low wall opposite the dark path. He needed to think about what he should do next, and where he ought to go.

Surely, he thought, *there must be someone in this strange new world that could make use of my talents, someone who was needful, and someone I can truly help.*

Before he'd hardly finished his thought a loud cry echoed from somewhere along the dark pathway. *'DANIEL!!'* it came. Dave turned to look and saw a small human with scruffy dark hair, grey trousers and a blue blazer come to a sudden stop on the grass verge.

"What, Mum?" the boy yelled back over his shoulder.

"How many times have I told you not to run across the road, Daniel? You'll be the death of me, you silly boy."

"Sorry, Mum."

"Now—look left and right and if there are no cars coming, WALK across the road."

The boy did as he was told and waved to a group of other small humans that were on the far side of the road.

Dave nodded to himself. *Ah!* he thought. *The dark pathway is called a road.* He made a note of this term. *Perhaps*, he continued to think, *that yellow box I saw is called a car*.

As Dave sat there, on the wall thinking his helpful thoughts, nobody walked by, and even when Dave looked up, and raised his hand to wave hello, Nobody just ignored him and carried on down the cracked and uncracked path, as if Dave did not exist—someone not worth bothering about.

"Oh well," Dave sighed. "This is surely a very strange world."

With nothing else to do he decided to relax and just watch this whole new world unfold in front of him; particularly as the weather had turned rather nice now that the sun had come out.

Dave took the Ray-Ban glasses from his pocket and put them on. Behind them he closed his eyes, whilst he absorbed the sun's rays, and he began to think about his life as it was before his miraculous change.

Chapter 14
A Child's Misery is Only Known to Them

"No! You can't look for them now. And, anyway, you should have put them away after you," the children's mother moaned at them. "How many times have I told you, 'you must put things away after you'?

"I've not been put on this earth to do the clearing up after you, every time you make a mess. Is that understood?" the children's mother finished berating them.

Hannah and Josephine knew what their mother was talking about, and they'd always tidied up after themselves, but this time this problem was not their fault.

They'd got their school satchels ready the night before, ready for their after school tuition. They knew what they had to do, it was the routine. Both of them had put their stuff on the *'Going out tomorrow evening for maths lessons'* cupboard shelf, after having a go on the PlayStation, but before going to bed. Their mother would've preferred them to do the things a different way around, but mixing up the order was the only way they had to be independent from their mother's rule.

Their mother's chiding was the last thing they'd expected when they'd arrived home from school. Their good day at school, the happy feelings they felt, just disappeared along with their smiles, as if their day's joy had been sucked out of them.

Hannah looked at her sister. "What did you do with the stuff?" she asked Josephine.

"Nothing!" Josephine moaned. She felt she was about to get the blame for everything.

"You're always doing this; trying to get us in trouble," her sister continued.

"No I'm not," Josephine said, almost in tears.

"Well, where are they then?" Hannah demanded.

"I don't know," Josephine said, shaking her head. "They were on the cupboard shelf. Honest. Han."

* * *

Dave opened his eyes shaking off the memories of his past. Something had brought him out of his daydreams. But what? Dave listened. On the breeze he heard anxious voices wafting through the air, from some window of some other huge house on the opposite side of the dark pathway. *ROAD!* he yelled at himself, in his head. He was sure he'd get it right soon.

As he looked towards the source of the voices he noticed two large white numbers on the front of the house, next to a door; they were a number four and a number two—42.

* * *

"Josephine," Hannah said, "I told you to put our stuff on the cupboard shelf."

"I did. *I did!*" moaned Josephine.

"Why aren't they there now then, Jo?"

"I don't know. Please don't be cross."

"Why don't you know?" Hannah said, ignoring her sister's pleas.

"You were with me, Han. We both did it."

Hannah had to admit Jo was right but how would she calm down her mother? She'd no idea, and was not looking forward to the discussion.

"Have you girls sorted out your books yet?" their mother asked again, calling up the stairs.

"No, Mum," Hannah had to say.

"Right. Girls. That's it. You know I'm going to have to cancel this evening's maths lesson. Do you know how much this is going to cost? I only pay for this to help you, you ungrateful pair."

Dave heard the whole conversation. He was not only uncomfortable at the sisters' plight but was also intrigued about how the situation had come to pass.

I'm going to do something about this, Dave thought. This situation, the plight of the two girls he'd heard, was exactly the reason he believed he'd been changed. Now no longer a simple feather (not that feathers were simple, just a bit dim, perhaps), he was in control. He could choose what he could do—he didn't need the featherdom to decide for him—he, Dave, would figure out why the voices he'd heard were so unhappy, and make their lives right.

No matter what it took, he'd be the brave one, the one crossing the dark path, (*ROAD!*) the one to rescue these poor people from the horribleness they were suffering.

He, Dave, would solve their problems because he was '*the helper of all needful people*'.

Dave smiled as he realised this was going to be his first test in the new and unpredictable world of the walking and talking.

Most people would have worried at the thought they needed to do something they'd never needed to do before. But Dave believed everything happened for a reason and, for him, being struck by a lightning bolt four times, and ending up with two feet and so much more, could only mean one thing—he was here to help, and help he would, whatever he needed to do.

Feet! Dave thought, a huge smile appeared on his face. He swung his legs back and forth and watched his boot clad feet swing in time with his legs.

He shook his head as another, different, thought crossed his mind. The reason he was here certainly had nothing to do with how awesome he looked in his new yellow bodysuit, his new gloves, and his new boots—that would be *really* mad! Although...

Chapter 15
Problems are Hard to Fix

Dave decided to make his way to number 42. He didn't know how he was going to get into the house or how he was going to fix the problem. But in his heart of hearts he knew, not only that he would help, but he could help, in some way or another. It was only the how, that was the problem, and this being the only problem, he felt sure it would solve itself—in some way.

He hopped off the wall he'd been sitting on and attempted to get to the house. Little did he know it was going to take a very long time. In fact it took him almost the entire day to get across the road to the house on the other side.

Each time he stepped onto the road, which lay between two grass verges, huge metallic-looking things growled passed him; Dave assumed these were the cars the mum human had warned the little human, Daniel, about. And every time they passed, Dave had to stop.

The multi-coloured, growling boxes were not something Dave felt he was up to tackling. He was sure they would win especially as they seemed to have an invisible power. As each metallic thing passed he felt the tug of a force that pulled him towards them, every time they whizzed by. It tried to suck him onto the road, and under their circular spinning discs of silver. It was only his strength, the grip his gloves gave him, and the long grass of the verge that enabled him to stop himself being whisked from the side of the road into their path.

This world was strange; these peculiar growling car-monsters were strange. The only difference between each of them, as far as he could tell, was their colour. They came in blues, browns, greens, blacks—actually Dave couldn't pick out a skin colour they didn't have. Each and every one of them was lifted above the ground by sets of black circles, with silvery bits at their centres.

And all the boxes had silver pipes sticking out from them, from what Dave assumed to be, the back of the box. He'd based his assumption on the direction the boxes were travelling. Dave had considered it very unlikely that the growling machines would be zooming anywhere, backwards.

It was from these pipes that the deep growling noise came as the boxes went by. And all of the multi-coloured boxes got in his way, or forced him to grab hold of anything he could just to save himself from being dragged onto the road when they zoomed past.

Dave looked up and down the road, shrugged his shoulders; none of this mattered. He, Dave, was going to get to the house, come what may.

I will make sure this strange force, whatever it is, will never beat me again, he told himself.

Another growling car-thing passed him and sucked him off his feet. Dave snatched yet another tuft of grass as he was lifted up, and started to fly through the air. He held tight.

As his body was dragged towards the road once more he shook his head. *Sometimes, I think, problems are just a little bit hard to fix. But this is not going to stop me*! Dave smiled. He was a very determined individual.

After a while, for some unknown reason, the road became quiet, no more growling cars zipped by, and Dave was able to cross the road without any further problems.

He followed the pavement on the other side of the road and strolled up to the door of the house numbered 42, then stared at it agog. The door was huge. Huger than any huge thing he'd come across before, except for an actual house.

If he was totally honest with himself this was the hugest thing he had ever encountered before—ever. Apart from the sky, he added as an afterthought. Oh! And the house, he added again.

Looking at the ginormous door it became obvious to him that he wouldn't be able to use this entrance, and, in fact, he needed to seek another way in, if he were going to help the troubled people he'd heard earlier.

Next to the door was a side passage, a side passage leading to the back of the house, he assumed. Just like the one he'd walked through when leaving Tariq's home.

Dave, being the decisive individual he was, now, decided to use the side passageway to see if it led to any other entrance that he could manage to use as an entrance. The passageway was dim due to the shadows created by the closely packed overhanging branches of trees and shrubs down one of its sides. The other side was the side of the house numbered 42. To top it all the barely risen morning sun failed to shed any light down the length of the passageway.

In his heart of hearts he knew he could help

Dave felt more comfortable using the passageway as he felt he was less obvious than the usual individuals that probably used this alley.

He was very conscious that he stuck out like a sore thumb, not because he was a sore thumb but because he was a feather, and a unique one at that, having an interesting pair of red boots and a very curious pair of gloves, attached to a bright yellow bodysuit, exactly as he did.

Dave looked around and then darted down the alleyway that ran alongside the house numbered 42.

Chapter 16
Pleasing One's Mother

The girls shared a bedroom and Hannah's bed was on the opposite side of the room to Jo's.

At the foot of Josephine's bed was the light-lemon coloured cupboard which contain the critical 'Going out tomorrow evening for maths lessons' shelf.

Hannah didn't have a cupboard at the foot of her bed, just a pine chest of drawers that she shared with her sister.

Beneath the only window in the room, the

one that overlooked the main road, was a small pine dresser with a framed mirror on its top. And scattered across that top were hair grips, brushes, rubber bands and all sorts of face cream, and some make-up.

Hannah sat on her bed and stared at Jo. She looked at her sister's straggly strawberry blonde hair as it wrapped around her freckled face, bob like.

Jo sat on her bed and stared at her sister. Her sister was her best friend and sometimes she wished she had Hannah's long and straight brunette hair; it always looked good. For a very brief moment Jo felt some happiness but then their mess came back to haunt her.

Both girls were miserable, and both had no idea how they were going to make their mother happy.

Neither of them knew how they'd got into the situation in the first place. Everything was so unfair.

Hannah knew in her heart she shouldn't have blamed her younger sister. Something had happened and whatever had caused it, none of it was their fault—this time. But, as usual, they'd got the blame anyway, and this time there was no way either of them could sort it out.

All of a sudden Jo's face lit up and she jumped off her bed. She'd had an idea.

"Hannah—let's look in the cupboard again. We might just have not seen where the maths books were. We didn't take them anywhere."

"Okay, Jo," Hannah said, hoping that everything was going to be all right. But everything inside her was telling her that neither of them had been mistaken, and both of them had missed their obvious dusky-orange coloured notebooks, and the glossy maths exercise books.

Jo made her way to the cupboard and Hannah stood up from her bed, then followed her younger sister across their bedroom's soft dusty pale-blue carpet.

As they stood in front of the room's only

cupboard both stared at its two doors and hoped the missing books were there, just not seen when they'd last opened it.

"You do it, Han," Jo implored. She thought that if she opened the door, herself, because it was her idea, then there'd be no hope of finding their books.

Hannah reached for the cupboard door. Then stopped. "I think you should do it, Jo. It's your idea."

Jo shook her head. "If I do it then the cupboard monster will make sure they're not there, Han. *Please?*"

"Cupboard monster? Where did you get *that* idea from?" Hannah laughed. Then instantly regretted it. Her sister was only trying to find a reason why the books should disappear.

"Don't laugh, Hannah. Something's taken our books." Tears started to well up in Jo's eyes.

"I'm sorry, Jo. I'm sure there's a reason. Just not a cupboard monster."

"Okay, Han. If you say so. But are you going to open it?" her sister implored.

Hannah complied with her little sister's wishes. She could see how upset Jo was. "Sure," Hannah said and pulled sharply on the doors' handles. The cupboard doors flew open and the sisters stared in.

Hannah shook her head. "Nope," she said.

Jo gazed into the cupboard. "Nope," she

agreed.

Not a thing had changed. The shelf they'd put their maths stuff on the previous day, was still empty.

Jo was crestfallen. Tears welled in her eyes, then began to trickle down her face, across her flushed cheeks. "Hannah, how are we going to make Mother happy? I've used up all my pocket money, and don't have any left to pay for more books," she sobbed.

"Neither do I," Hannah said, misery making her voice crack a little.

"What are we going to do, Han? I don't like this. This is horrible."

Hannah put an arm around her sister's

shoulder and pulled her close. "I'll think of something. I'm sure it'll work out."

"Really, Han? You're really going to work it out?"

"Of course," Hannah lied. What was she to do? She truly didn't know. What else could she say? Jo was her little sister and her little sister needed to know that things always worked out—she wasn't old enough to know the truth.

Chapter 17
Journey of Discovery

The passage way finished at the rear of the property and overlooked a fairly long garden.

At its head, opposite the passageway and next to a small concrete patio, that extended a little way into the garden, was a broken down garden shed. The shed leant to the left, so much so its door didn't fit its frame, and because of this it was kept shut with an old piece of frayed rope.

At the left hand side of the crooked shed was

an equally crooked fence which ran the length of the garden. Both shed and fence were made from, what seemed to be, wooden panels so ancient the sun-bleached wood had an '*almost-grey*' type colour.

At the furthest end of the garden an unkempt vegetable patch could be seen. It was bordered by long and uncut grass on every side. At its centre beige-brown bamboo canes clambered skyward from the soil, tied together at their tops, to make a frame for peas or tomatoes to climb; though the plant that had wrapped itself around the canes, and had made them its home, was neither.

In the rear wall of the house was another

seemingly impossible entrance type thing, just like the one at the front. But this one was different. This entrance had a small square hole cut into it, near its base. The hole was covered by some kind of see-through material, which flapped back and forth in the light afternoon breeze.

A single paved step led from the patio up to the back door and its flap-like opening.

Okay. This is it, Dave thought. *This is my way to get in*.

Dave jumped up onto the back step. He reached forward and pushed the flap open, then let it swing shut.

Dave's heart was thumping; this was *sooo*

something he'd never ever done before, and he doubted that any of his kind had done this before: Thinking about it he *knew* none of his kind had ever done this before. Even so, he still had a mission to accomplish, and accomplish it he would.

He pushed the flap open once more and pulled himself through the hole and fell straight into the house.

Dave stood up and looked around. There were vague outlines of things, but he really couldn't make anything out in the dim room. It was like some kind of strange dark veil had stopped him from seeing the room properly, almost as if a mysterious shroud had fallen from nowhere to cloud his sight. As Dave pondered the situation he lifted his Ray-Bans from his face and scratched his head. All of a sudden the room's dimensions and interior became clear—visible. Dave held the Ray-Ban sunglasses out in front of him and studied them. *Interesting*, he thought. To make sure his theory was correct he put his sunglasses back on, and sure enough, the room dimmed and the room's cupboards and furniture returned to vague outlines.

A knowing smile crossed his face as he removed the Ray-Bans and put them in his pocket. *These Ray-Bans could be very useful in certain circumstances,* he thought, but didn't know how or when. He just knew they would.

He looked around the room once more. *That's better*, he thought further.

To either side of him were many more doors, but ones that were much smaller and whiter than the one at the front of the house. He decided to ignore them and carry on, and go deeper into the depths of the house; it was not the small doors in this room that needed him. But somewhere in this mysterious placed there were individuals who did.

He left the room of many doors, albeit small ones, and entered a corridor; it was time to make another decision. There was an exit to his left, something he could follow, or straight on along the corridor.

Because Dave was not so sure he truly knew his left from his right, mainly because it was only recently that he'd acquired arms—one on the left and one on the right—he thought it best to go straight on. So he did.

At the end of the corridor he came across another huge entrance that looked exactly the same as the huge entrance he'd seen from the front of the house, on the outside, but this time its crafted contours were inset, totally opposite to what he'd viewed from the outside.

Behind him lay a huge cliff-like cliff of white painted wood and beige carpet; it consisted of regular short, flat and upright risers connected by similarly short and flat horizontal ones.

In his mind's eye he could see the open window he'd looked towards whilst he'd sat on the low wall, earlier that day.

Dave knew he had to climb this peculiar, regular, cliff face to get to where he needed to go. And as soon as he'd achieved this he would be able to start his investigation into the problems of the humans he'd decided were children—something he was sure would be verified: he'd heard them, and their problems; everything that had drifted across the road from the upstairs window and had entered his ears.

Without a pause up the peculiar cliff he went. Getting to the top was a hard slog but being Dave he managed it.

As he struggled from the final step of the staircase onto the landing he was presented with three options, left, forward or right.

Still uncertain of his left or right he started to use his nose and sniffed, deeply. There was a tang in the air he recognised from his time sitting on the wall along the road when he'd heard the poor girls' exclamations. He turned to his right and strolled into the room he'd heard the children's worrying coming from.

Directly in front of him, on either side of the room, was a bed, each one had a young girl sitting on it. Each girl looked at the other in such a lost way Dave felt moved and his heart went out to them.

Dave knew then he'd got to the right place. Dave also knew that the job he had to do was not going to be easy.

Without warning the children's mother's voice cut through the air. Dave shuddered.

"Girls... come here now. We're going out."

Dave dived, as fast as he could, behind the low chest of drawers on his left, (not that he knew it was his left for definite but for the purposes of this story it was clear!).

Both girls walked passed him, heads hung low, towards and then down the peculiar cliff or stairs as he was to find out later.

Suddenly there was a huge bang followed by a growl which Dave now associated with the metallic things that ran about on tracks of concrete using circular rubber circle things. Dave was now alone in the girls' bedroom. Or so he thought!

Now, Dave said to himself, *let's see what the problem is*.

He wandered around the room, looking high, looking low, and looking from side to side.

"Oh blinkin' flittery-bug," he swore. It was becoming apparent he didn't have a feather's chance in a tornado to work out, or even determine, any way he could solve the problem.

Some detective I'm turning out to be, some helper of needful people I am, Dave chided himself.

He sat down on the floor in between the kid's beds looking at the carpet for inspiration, and started to ponder.

There was a sudden movement across the room; a CD flew by seemingly propelled by nothing.

Dave missed the flying CD incident as he was still staring at the floor seeking an idea that would help him get to the bottom of the problem.

How was he ever going to cheer up the kids? How was he going to sort out their problem? Did happiness come from being able to go to maths lessons? He felt it probably didn't but in this case it certainly did. Was he right to get involved? Yes, because it was his destiny to be the helper of needful people. Did he have any clue about what to do next? No.

That's an interesting bit of fluff, thought Dave as he continued staring at the carpet. *I wonder why it's blue?*

Chapter 18
Poltergeists? Don't Be Stupid

The Movitall was having another good day. Yesterday had been pretty successful. No one had noticed it whilst it had moved all the maths books from the lemon coloured cupboard, rolled them up, then stuffed them down the centre of the toilet rolls in the bathroom.

The Movitall knew that today was going to be just the same—another good day—it was looking forward to the tricks it had planned for the two children, and perhaps their mother, if it had enough time during its examination.

The Movitall was having a good day

But then it had second thoughts about performing tricks on the mother. The Movitall thought it could be marked down, if it involved the mother in the practical exam, because the exam it was taking was the **G**hostly **C**ertification in **S**caring **E**veryone, **G**eneral **H**aunting **of S**choolkids and **T**eachers—Level 1.

The mother was not a teacher, and certainly not a school kid. So after a brief pause the Movitall decided not to trick the mother. But, perhaps another day, when it was taking its GCSE in Distressing Elders, Mothers and Other Nice-people exams; the GCSE DEMON ones, it would come back and put as much fear into the mother as it could.

Above all else the one thing the Movitall wanted to be was the best in its year. Little did it know that its goal was going to be delayed until the next academic year.

The Movitall had watched the mother and the two girls leave the house and get into one of those noisy, stinky cars, and then drive off. It knew it was now free to move the other stuff, which was listed on the GHoST level 1 practical exam paper, without being interrupted.

Not even the annoying rag bag cat, which had mooched about the day before, had protested enough to raise the alarm. But knowing cats was that unusual? The Movitall didn't think so.

It was very certain that soon, after these exams, the exams it would have to pass, it would achieve fully fledged poltergeistdom and then be allowed to haunt any house it wished, for a small fee of course; thus letting it earn its way in the lands of the living.

The Movitall floated above the landing and along the short, beige carpeted hallway, past the mother's room, as it made its way to the sisters' bedroom.

The Movitall looked at both the girls' beds and wondered which one it should dishevel first, which one needed to be messed up the most.

Then it remembered the younger sister talking about a cupboard monster and how the elder sister had dismissed the idea of monsters. So it made its decision. It would "work" on the eldest sister's bed first. That would teach her; that would let her know that there were such things as monsters, and ghosts and Boogey Men, and even Poltergeists and Movitalls.

And, perhaps, because of this decision and the way it had made its choice, it would score higher points in its GHoST level 1 practical exam—because it had chosen the human that had deserved to be tricked the most.

And so the Movitall dived out of the air down onto Hannah's bed and heaved the duvet from it, then threw it up into the air allowing it to fall back to the floor in a crumpled heap. As the duvet *flomped* onto the floor dust and fluff was puffed about the room.

Although the Movitall had noticed Dave sitting on the girls' bedroom floor it had assumed he was just a strange shaped toy. This was because Dave hadn't moved once during the Movitall's floaty trickery. Dave had been too absorbed in his own thoughts, about the blue fluff, to notice that things were going on around him. But for a being recently changed from an inanimate, unmoving, un-walking feather into a feather with attitude, legs, feet, a bum, and lots of other stuff that feathers did not usually have, it wasn't surprising that this new individual was a little preoccupied—the world around it was huge, not understandable, but mostly interesting.

However, very soon, Dave and the Movitall—the poltergeist in training—were going to become very aware of each other.

Chapter 19
A Hero in the Making

Dave had felt this sensation before, when he'd been flying in the air above the countryside. But, this time, when he looked down it wasn't the countryside he could see; all he could see was a light blue carpet a metre or so beneath him, nothing more, no trees or sheep or rivers to look down upon.

Whilst he'd been thinking about the strange blue fluff, without being aware, somehow he'd become airborne.

But how could this be? He studied the floor and saw a duvet lying there, crumpled on the floor beneath him.

Floating about in the air was nothing unusual for Dave the Feather, but suddenly being grappled by the heavy and rough hands of gravity was an entirely new experience. Gravity had never taken much notice of him, and the Jonesy Featherdom, in his previous life as seventh of two hundred and eighteen thousand, three hundred and ninety four. But it seemed things had changed, quite a lot in fact.

"Oooo, that tickles!" exclaimed Dave.

"Oh! Sorry. My fault," Gravity said in a low bass voice as it adjusted its grip on him.

Dave began to make his way back towards the girls' carpet in a feather's typical floaty fashion—rocking back and forth in the air like a child's crib would, if it wasn't in the air and had been pushed by the hand of a mother, who was attempting to encourage her baby to sleep after a mid-morning feed.

His descent back towards the floor's carpet was not a straight forward affair. In fact the air circulating the room pushed him towards the girls' chest of drawers, where he'd hidden earlier. And as he floated towards the bedroom furniture he began to think that there was something not quite right about his floating. The more he thought about it the more he felt it was really wrong—somehow undesired. *But why?* his mind asked. Dave shrugged and shook his head. He didn't have an answer for his mind.

But then, out of nowhere, the reason became crystal clear; and it was a simple one. It was because he'd not started to float in the air through his own choice or effort.

In his previous life the decision to float—or fly as it was called in the days when he'd been an ordinary feather—was started by Jonesy and only after Jonesy made the decision to float did the Jonesy Featherdom work, all at the same time, to float and then fly, taking Jonesy into the air.

However, as Dave considered his new

circumstance, he decided that this was, perhaps, a normal turn of events in the new world he had now become a part of, and him being of his kind.

As soon as he'd reached the floor he jumped to his feet, then bent his knees and held his hands out in front of him, in the exact manner a karate expert wouldn't.

He turned his head quickly from left and then to the right as he looked around the room, there was nothing. He couldn't see a thing—not one reason why the duvet would float up into the air and then flop back down. Although the reason for it coming down was obvious to him. It was the reason why it had got up, in the first place, that he couldn't figure out.

All the windows were closed, closed because the girls had shut them before they'd left with their mother. There was no breeze at all, let alone one that would be strong enough to blow the duvet into the air and then onto the floor.

Then, all of a sudden, there was another movement, one Dave managed to catch out of the corner of his eye. He turned to face it. Again weird stuff was happening with one of the beds. Dave watched as a pillow, on the eldest girl's bed, levitate itself, and then with a determined effort, throw itself onto the floor, in what seemed to be a huff, just in the same way the duvet had apparently done.

These happenings were beyond Dave's normal areas of expertise. In his experience he knew about everything that could float, fly and glide. But what he'd just witnessed was beyond anything he'd seen before; beyond anything he knew about.

He realised he needed to take some time to study what was going on. But this time, from a place that was safe; one that would mean he was safe from becoming accidentally airborne again, at the very least. The choice was simple. He made his way back to the rear of the girls' chest of drawers.

Once out of harm's way he pushed a gloved hand into one of his incredibly deep pockets. He hoped he'd been given something that would help him with his investigation into the strange happenings the two sisters were experiencing. Whether it be from Tariq, or the strange force that had made him more person than feather. He hoped that his electrification process had not only given him some excellent sunglasses but also information in some form or another.

Within a second his hand landed upon, what seemed to be, a book of some kind. He pulled on the heavy rectangular object in his pocket, an object that felt it was made of paper, and one having four clear sides.

As he pulled the object from his pocket it came out with a pop sound. It was the same sound as if someone had plucked air from their cheek, by putting their forefinger into their mouth and, using the tip of their finger, pulling it across the inside of their cheek.

He looked at what he held in his hand. The cover read, 'The Sterling Encyclopaedia of Unexplained Events'.

Dave nodded to himself. This was exactly the thing he needed. He thumbed rapidly through the tome. He was looking for any entry that mentioned 'levitating bedware'.

But no sooner he'd started, he'd stopped. He looked at his bright-red gloved hand. *A THUMB!* he thought to himself, and chuckled. *What an amazing world this is*, he thought further, then continued to flick through the book as he looked for something that would help him in his quest to solve the mystery of the girls' missing maths books.

To Dave's surprise, and dismay, the encyclopaedia stopped at 'bed' and continued with 'car'. No 'bedware' entry, levitating or otherwise, was to be found between 'bed' and 'car'.

Why Dave had made the decision to borrow this huge and heavy book from Tariq he had no idea. But then it was something Tariq had given him—a sign of friendship he'd assumed. But, so far, it had been a totally pointless exercise; the information contained within the book not helping at all. He returned the encyclopaedia back to one of his impossibly deep pockets.

Chapter 20
The Problem with Understanding the Problem is Understanding the Problem

His pocket easily absorbed the encyclopaedia.

What to do now? he wondered. After careful consideration and thought, with a little thinking thrown in, Dave decided to move just far enough behind the chest of drawers to observe all that was going on, or not as the case may be, without being seen himself. Then, as he watched the room, he hoped inspiration, that small spark of an idea, would appear in his head and take him a little closer to solving the problem of the girls' missing maths books.

Dave shuffled back behind the drawers, sat down and crossed his legs and waited.

Not unsurprisingly, to anyone who knew what was going on, another of the girls' belongings no longer wanted to be stationary and lifted itself from the sideboard, straight up into the air, then floated towards Hannah's bed. Once above it, it dropped onto the quilt, bounced a couple of times then became the stationary object it should always have been. This time around it was the turn of the portable CD player.

Dave peeked out from the back of the chest

of drawers. It was clear his new position was really not one that would afford him any better information about the nature of the problem he was attempting to solve. Without a doubt he needed to get a better view of the comings and goings of the usually inanimate, unmoving objects.

He looked up towards the top of the drawers and in that instant knew that the top of the chest would probably be the best place to have a lookout. He started to climb. One hand at a time he grabbed at the corner of the chest of drawers; gloved hand over gloved hand he pulled himself up, stretching and straining as he did.

There seemed to be a special grip in his mighty red gloves, a grip that stopped him from slipping back to the blue fluffy carpet below. The fact he was also as light as a feather helped as well.

Once he'd reached the top he was certain he'd get a clear view of all that was happening, and once he did he would be able to decide on the actions he would need to take next.

Dave pushed, and for the fifth time a gloved hand reached out above his head, and this time his fingertips felt a sharp angle and a level surface. It was the top of the chest of drawers— at last. He threw his other hand up and pulled himself onto the top. Without pausing he made his way to its centre.

More cautious about being spotted and the cause of the objects' strange movements, he didn't check his footing as he scuttered across the chest's wooden top. His only interest being to determine the cause of the movement of the girls' things; where he stepped was of much less importance. Or so he thought.

In his path, open and lying on the chest's wooden surface, was a pencil case made from blue denim-like material, minding its own business as most do, with its contents, namely rulers, rubbers, superglue and pencils, strewn across the chest's top.

To Dave's sudden surprise his balance went

helter-skelter. His arms wind-milling in an attempt to save himself from toppling over.

He'd stepped on one of the pencils, which had shot out from beneath his foot in a westerly direction. His arms continued to wind-mill in the vain hope the action would steady his unstable stance.

But, unfortunately, his automatic response to falling over had no effect whatsoever. With his balance finally lost he sat down heavily on a carelessly placed tube of Superglue. The force of his landing on the tube of glue squirted its contents across the chest top and under the pencil case. Being superglue, and as it should, it immediately stuck fast the pencil case to the top of the chest of drawers.

Dave sighed with relief. He'd just narrowly missed becoming part of a sticky and gluey sculpture made from a feather, a pencil case and its scattered contents. Now it was made from only the pencil case and its contents.

If I were an artist, Dave wondered, *how much would I get for that?* He smiled at his thought then shook his head. There were many more important things to be thinking and doing. He dismissed the thought and decided that focusing on the task at hand was the more appropriate course of action.

After checking the coast was clear he stood up, then carried on across the chest's top. On its far side was a jam jar. In it were a few stems of Tulip that were looking a little worse for wear, and certainly the water needed to be changed. Its murky nature and limey green colour indicating it was way past its sell-by date. It was beside the opaque jam jar he felt he would get the best view of the goings on.

Once behind the jam jar he made himself comfortable, and waited to see if any other events would unfold—hopefully giving him further clues as to the nature of the girls' book problem.

Chapter 21
Exams can be Troublesome

After its efforts the Movitall was pleased with the successes it'd had—the kid's duvet, the CDs, the CD player and all the rest of the girls' stuff, especially their maths books. Everything it'd tried had worked. But this didn't stop the Movitall worrying about its pass mark. Although pleased with what it had achieved it had to pause; the GCSE practical exam was exhausting. It tested all the skills the Movitall had been taught during its final year at

Poltergeist University.

The Movitall bobbed up and down, in a floaty fashion, as it rested in the top left hand corner of the girls' room. From this position, not visible to anyone, it could watch the results of its actions unfold.

Although the Movitall had completed all preparations needed for the practical exam, it still went over its next steps. No matter how much it had prepared, now it was in the actual practical exam, its nerves threatened to get the better of it.

As it had left the grounds of Poltergeist University, to float its way to the house it had been assigned for its practical exam, the

Movitall had glided past other undergraduates who were not interested in taking the exam, they had other ideas. Those students had hid in cubby-holes and alcoves, anywhere where shadows prevailed. And as the unsuspecting pupils passed those dark places they'd been approached by the way-ward students as they tried to push remedies for nerves, preparations to enhance memory, and even guides on how to pass the practical exam.

Although tempted the Movitall had resisted. It knew, if it was going to pass its GCSE, it would do it itself and not by using anything that was on offer. The Movitall believed it would not get any satisfaction from passing its exam, if it had done so by cheating the system—as a Movitall youngster it remembered being taught by its parents, '*Nothing is worth having unless it means effort, pain and difficulty.*'

The Movitall knew it had time to change its plan, if it was necessary. It would adjust any and every step, in fact, do anything to make sure it would get the scores necessary to pass its GCSE, the most important exam of its entire life, the Ghostly Certification in Scaring Everyone.

Time ticked away, and time tocked away. Then from nowhere came a voice. But not a little voice that would have appeared to be a lonesome whisper, but A LOUD VOICE that

BOOMED.

If the Movitall hadn't been a ghost, studying to be a poltergeist, its sudden jump at the unexpected interruption would have meant it would have bruised its head very painfully.

Fortunately, at the loud interruption to its thoughts, although it did jump, it simply passed through the girls' bedroom ceiling, before floating back to where it started from; the top right hand corner of the girls' room.

"WELL, YOUNG MOVITALL," bellowed the Voice of Mystery from the Netherworld. "You're on your final test. SO DON'T FORGET THE FOUR PRINCIPLES OF OTHERWORLDLINESS YOU WILL BE JUDGED UPON."

It was a mystery to the Movitall why its tutors always had to shout out instructions, but after three years of being at Poltergeist University it had become used to the approach.

"Master, Voice of Mystery from the Netherworld, would you tell me so I may check my notes?" the Movitall asked.

"Your notes, young Movitall, should reflect the following key points of your final exam. It is not in my remit to ask why they apparently don't.

"You will be judged on the following criteria, just as the candidates of Poltergeist University have always been," the Voice of Mystery from the Netherworld answered, before declaring the details.

"Damageeeee," the Master boomed with the uttered word eventually fading away until it became inaudible in the room. "Styleeeee," The Master's voice continued, in its strange trailing off manner. "Controlll...lll. And aggression," The Master finished.

To ensure the young student Movitall was completely clear on the points the Master had made, The Master elaborated further.

"Damage; this will be judged upon how much of it you can inflict on the humans' credibility. How much you can take away other human's belief in them."

The Voice of Mystery from the Netherworld

paused for a moment, and allowed the Movitall time to absorb the point—even though a student, like any other, it should have already learnt the lesson. But the Voice of Mystery was happy to allow some flexibility in the examination process—so few Movitalls took up haunting the living these days, something had to be done.

The Master continued to expound the definitions of the principles followed by those of the *Otherworld*, the world of Movitalls, Poltergeists, Masters and Headless Masters, to name just a few of its inhabitants.

The Voice of Mystery from the Netherworld felt it needed to make sure the student Movitall understood the level of skill it had to attain, to become a fully-fledged poltergeist.

"Style," it continued its education. "This will be judged upon the flare and panache and elegance used to inflict damage on the human's believability.

"Control; this will be judged upon how you execute your style.

"And finally—aggression. This will be judged upon how scarily you manage to achieve the previous three objectives of the exam."

The Movitall had managed moving and concealing the school books, it had moved a pillow; it had moved a duvet, a CD and a CD player, all of which were done impressively, if the Movitall had anything to admit to itself; and not forgetting the maths books.

What next? What next? the Movitall thought to itself. It wanted a high score for its practical exam.

Thinking back on its achievements with the school books, particularly as that had produced immense stress and misery in a certain few of the house's occupants, what could it do next? The duvet tactic had been a good demonstration, as had been the CD and the CD player, but that hadn't nor would cause any particular extra strife.

So what next? If the school books were good then what else?... Ah! Yes, the pencils and pens, actually everything that could be used to write. Now that must be the final choice, and in that choice the Movitall figured that it must achieve its best score yet.

Taking a deep breath the Movitall decided to go for the pencil case because, without the books, the kids could not do maths, but without the pencil case and the pencils the kids would not be able to do anything at school. So they would not just miss one lesson they would miss the whole curriculum!

That's what I'm going for, the Movitall decided and with the decision made the Movitall floated towards the pencil case on the top of the girls' dresser.

Chapter 22
Sideways Thinking

Dave continued to observe the goings on as he sat behind the jam jar on the top of the girls' chest of drawers. No matter how hard he tried, no matter how hard he thought, no matter how hard he wished, nothing entered his head. Not one single clue as to what was happening to these two poor girls presented itself.

All he knew was that he couldn't see a thing—just the items that had floated by, propelled by something he couldn't understand.

So much for my detective skills, he thought to himself. Dave was unhappy. He'd believed, very sincerely, that he'd been put on Earth to help the needful folk, just like the two girls who needed his help right now. But he wasn't helping in any way. As he'd been sat there, and looked across the bedroom, he'd seen CDs flying about, CD players moving, but no reason for it to happen.

Dave scrunched his mouth as he stared into the distance trying to figure out the next step he should take. He shook his head—there was nothing apparent.

Another item flew past him. Once again as if propelled by nothing. Dave watched its path.

After it hit the wall and fell to the floor he shook his head once more; there was just no explanation.

Without reason a thought started to grow in his head. Dave wasn't aware at first; the thought grew of its own accord. Like a little bulb sprouting shoots, eventually to become a big lightbulb that would go *plink* above his head as it switched on.

Now, after recently coming into existence, Dave found that a lot of things happened to him completely out of his control. Even ideas.

Sometimes he missed the comfort of the featherdom and how thoughts had happened. Never feeling alone when they came, feeling a shared responsibility for the thoughts as they popped from nowhere, like a balloon exploding backwards—*GNAB!* Millions of little unknown bits coming together, sticking together, to make a huge pink balloon filled to the brim with an idea. But not any longer. Not like now, when he was the one and only, the only one responsible for the thoughts, even if he had no idea where they came from.

Dave decided to let this particular thought stretch and grow, expand in his head. After a few seconds he thought he'd heard a *plink* sound.

All of a sudden it was clear and in his head Dave had figured this, *If there is anything going on that I cannot see, then what I'm looking for must be invisible.*

Dave nodded to himself at the thought's beginning. He liked where it was going so he let the thought grow a little more. *If what I'm looking for is invisible, then it must also be see-through, because that would make it invisible.* He nodded again and this time smiled as well. So he continued to follow the line of reasoning and thought. *To see through things you need a particular piece of equipment, something very special; something that allows you to see through things, something like X-Ray glasses perhaps?*

However, the thought in his head continued,

what I'm looking for is already invisible and that means I can see through it. So, for me to be able to see the see-through thing, in other words, for me to see something I can't, then I need, at the very least, some glasses that could un-see-through things that are see-through.

Which can only mean, Dave thought excitedly, *that I need some un-X-Ray glasses! A pair of glasses which are absolutely normal in every way.*

Dave put his hand into his pocket and reached for the Ray-Bans Tariq had given him earlier. He put on the ordinary-in-every-way glasses, the un-X-ray glasses and peaked out from behind the jam jar. He nearly fell off the dresser. He was totally astounded by the result.

The problem, all of a sudden, had become visible.

Chapter 23
To Achieve One's Goal You Must Succeed

The Movitall, the young undergraduate poltergeist, knew what it had to do; the final step that would guarantee its passing of the practical exam, the last test of the GCSE in Poltergeistdom.

It had rested enough, and after being prompted by The Voice of Mystery from The Netherworld, it started on its next steps.

After taking a deep breath the Movitall

floated towards the girls' open pencil case without a care. The Movitall had no option, the next things it did had to be done with confidence because, not only would it be judged on what it did, but also on how it did it.

The Movitall had decided on the pencil case as its object of choice for the practical exam, because if it moved the pencil case, and placed it somewhere other than where it should be, it was bound to get the highest marks ever; for the sole reason that hiding it would cause the most amount of grief and misery for the two girls, with the added effect of annoying the mother—a bonus.

Not only would the two girls not be able to do

Maths, but they wouldn't be able to do English, or Art, or Geography, or Science, or anything. Apart from P.E., of course, which was not a bad thing.

The Movitall smiled to itself barely able to hold in a chuckle. *And wouldn't that be just great?* it thought.

The girls would have to do P.E. for morning lessons, P.E. for mid-morning lessons, P.E. for afternoon lessons, P.E. all the time, all day long; and all because they didn't have anything to write or draw with.

They may be able to get out of P.E. once or twice, with a note from their mother, but that would be it.

The Movitall swiftly patted itself on the back. This was it. This would be the final pass it required to get its GCSE in Poltergeistdom. The Movitall was so happy. This was going to be so simple; a doddle—little did it know what was coming.

It took another huge breath and drew itself up to full height ready for the final pounce. As it lunged towards the pencil case it recalled the Voice of Mystery's instructions about the four principles of otherworldliness. The values the practical exam would be marked on.

Damage; well the Movitall had certainly got that licked—the girls were going to be so unhappy, so emotionally damaged—so unbelievable if they tried telling anyone.

"Cool," thought the Movitall

Every morning, as they walked through the school gates, and realised they'd be having yet another load of double P.E. lessons, they were sure to be struck with deep misery and sadness. And if their teachers asked them why they were so sad the Movitall knew they'd be laughed at, as they tried to explain to their teachers why they hadn't any pens or pencils.

Style; the Movitall did a quick loop the loop with a half twist. Then added a skilful leg movement by flicking its scrawny leg backward, bending it at the knee so the heel of its foot almost touched its bum. As it did so, it flicked back its head and lifted its left arm in a graceful arc across the front of its fanged face, as if it was going to brush its wispy green hair with the back of its hand. Hair that looked more like a wobbly, jelly-like, greeny-grey blob; almost like the ice cream on the top of an ice cream cone, but one you wouldn't want to eat; especially one that had a foggy-mist rising from it, leaving wispy green trails in the air every time the Movitall floated this way or that.

Control; the Movitall repeated its last movement only a lot more slowly this time.

And *aggression*; the Movitall grinned in an extremely manic fashion, its eyes open wide, showing all its grimy teeth, and its horribly yellow two long fangs—this was only show for the Mystery Voice from The Netherworld as no one living, in the bedroom, could actually see it.

Then it plucked out its own eyes with a pitch

fork it had just made appear in its right hand.

That's so cool! thought the Movitall. And it

smiled. For the last time.

Chapter 24
For the Want of an Unstuck Pencil Case

Dave didn't know what to do, especially now, as he could see the cause of the problem; one that had been so harrowing and misery making for the two young girls.

Dave shuddered as he saw a pitch fork appear in the thingamajig's hand. He quickly removed his Ray-Bans just in time to miss the floaty being shove the pitch fork into its eyes. Dave ducked back behind the murky jam jar to consider his options.

For a moment he sat in silence as he waited for another idea to backwards explode into his mind. But before it could Dave was disturbed by the sound of deep and heavy breaths, coming from the other side of the jam jar.

He peered around the jar. His mouth dropped open. The top of the blue pencil case, the part not stuck to the dresser, was moving violently back and forth, up and down.

What on Earth is..., Dave's thought started. Then he picked up his un-X-ray glasses and slapped them back on.

What he saw was the what-d'you-call-it puffing and panting, pulling and pushing, lifting and heaving, and looking around wildly, in a very worried way. It seemed that the what-ever-it-was was not at all happy and, all the while, getting more and more desperate as the pencil case decided to stay exactly where it was.

"Ooohhhhhhh nnnooooo!" wailed the Movitall in an omnipresent way.

"Ooohhhhhhh nnnooooo!" wailed Dave, shuddering as the Movitall's low and mournful moan vibrated through his body and everything around him.

Dave decided to play it safe and removed his Ray-Bans once more, then stuck his fingers in his ears. Peeking out from the corner of his eye he kept a check on the wobbling pencil case.

"No, no, no," the Movitall bellowed at the top of its voice. "This cannot be happening. You cannot be serious," the Movitall implored to no one in particular.

It just didn't know what to do. All its plans, every step it had worked out, just everything, had gone wrong.

What was wrong with this pencil case? Why didn't it move? How was he going to get his final pass? the Movitall wondered, and stopped. It sat down hard on the case.

As Dave watched the blue pencil case it stopped its wobble; and, for no apparent reason, its top sunk just as if it had been sat upon.

Dave removed his fingers from his ears and put his Ray-Bans back on. What he now saw was a very upset apparition. Its chin cupped by both its hands. Elbows on its knees. Seated on the top of the denim pencil case. And it was muttering something to itself.

Dave decided he needed to hear whatever it was the apparition was saying. He hoped its mutterings would help him resolve the situation for the two girls. But to do this he had to be quite a lot nearer to the muttering ghoul than he was at the moment.

Dave tiptoed from around the back of the jam jar, then softly shuffled towards a CD rack, which was just behind the pencil case the apparition sat upon.

"What am I going to do now? What AM I going to do?" the Movitall continued to groan to itself.

BING! A light bulb appeared from nowhere above the Movitall's head. In fact the Movitall had just made it appear itself. It wanted to show to the Voice of Mystery from the Netherworld, that although it had a slight problem, it was still more skilful than its classmates.

It had had a new idea. The light bulb plinked out of existence only to be replaced by a puff of swirling blue-grey smoke.

Uh-huh, the Movitall said to itself, and nodded as it smiled at its new cunning plan.

Dave was getting nearer; once he'd passed the CD rack he would be right behind the thing, and then would be able to hear every single word it muttered. He continued to watch it very carefully as he crept forward.

In an instant a frown of puzzlement leapt onto his eyebrows. The thing had now started doing, what could only be described as, squat thrusts; bending its knees, squatting down then stretching up and standing on tip toe. With each squat and thrust the Movitall sped up. Faster and faster it went. Up and down it pumped.

Dave was now concerned, very concerned— it looked like the weird apparition was about to do something very, very serious. At that moment Dave decided it wouldn't be a very good idea to stay where he was. As quietly as he could he retreated back to the safety of the murky jar of limp tulip stems.

Behind the jar once more he slowly peered out at the apparition, holding onto the jar with one hand, ready to pull himself back as quickly as he could, should the need arise. He was soon to find out that this was a particularly bad idea.

The Movitall, with every squat, mumbled to itself, *I'm going to do it. I'm going to do it. I'm REALLY going to do it.*

The Movitall's new idea was about using its momentum. The idea that once it had built up enough speed then that speed, and its weight, alone, would give it the ability to make all movement it needed free from resistance. And then it would be able to pull the, resistance free, pencil case from the top of the chest of drawers. And from that moment on its problem would be solved.

The Movitall had gone over every last part of its previous manoeuvre in its head. It had analysed everything it had done to achieve the goal of grabbing the pencil case, so it could move it to some other part of the house; a part of the house no one would think to look in.

Just as it had done with the maths books, each and every one being rolled up and stuffed neatly down the centre of unused toilet rolls in the bathroom, it would also move the pencil case to its allotted spot, which was a bag of self-raising flour in one of the kitchen's cupboards.

Obviously the whole point of the exercise was not to get rid of the items, but just move them to a place somewhere where the un-deceased wouldn't be able to discover them until later; somewhere where the misplaced items would, eventually, be found. Found in a place exactly where they ought not be; most definitely in the last place that any of the un-deceased would look. Maths books in the centre of unused toilet rolls, keys in the freezer, socks in the microwave, cat in the tumble dryer, dogs in next door's kids' sandpit, and pencil cases in bags of self-raising flour, and so on and so forth.

The Movitall had spent weeks remembering every place for every item. All of these places were detailed in a book that was central to a Movitall's education; a huge yellow book with large black lettering on its front. It was called, 'Poltergeistdom for Ghoulies'.

With two further squats and thrusts the Movitall made an almighty leap into the air. Up went the Movitall and it moved very fast. This move caused a gap in the air; a hole where the Movitall had just been. The gap, needing to be filled, sucked air from the surroundings into the void the Movitall had left and, unfortunately for Dave, it sucked him into it as well.

Dave found himself in the process of levitating once again and made a swift grab for the jam jar, attempting to grasp it with both hands.

He missed the jar completely, but just about managed to snatch the top of one of the tulips, only for it to topple the jam jar with the tulip falling from his hand. Dave was left grasping thin air, and was drawn up into the uncontrolled vortex of spinning air left in the Movitall's wake.

The jar fell to its side and spilt its smelly, limey green, watery contents across the top of the chest of drawers; the few stems of tulip the jar contained were thrown across the dresser's top. Some skidded from the top onto the girls' bedroom floor.

Not much longer after, a puddle of slimy water started to trickle towards the blue pencil case. Within seconds the pencil case was soaked and the glue, sticking it to the top of the chest of drawers, was loosened.

"Whhhooaaahhhh," yelled Dave as he hurtled upwards, caught in the thingamajig's slip stream.

"Yea haaaaa," went the Movitall, as it slid silently to a halt in the air, and prepared for its final plunge downwards, towards the pencil case.

ZOOM. Off went the Movitall, as fast as it could, in its attempt to finish its level 2 module, of the GCSE Poltergeistdom examination.

"Aaaaagrraaahhh!" the Movitall exclaimed as it noticed a strange chestnut brown feather, wearing a look of horror and some silly red gloves, hurtling towards it. What had surprised the Movitall the most was that the feather thing was hurtling towards it, at almost the same speed, it was travelling towards the brown feather itself.

The Movitall blinked twice and revised its observation, a strange brown feather wearing a look of horror, a skin tight yellow body suit, some silly red gloves and a particularly nice pair of Ray-Ban shades!

Dave braced himself for the massive impact,

certain of his imminent demise.

Oh well, Dave thought. *This has certainly been different from what I've been used to. Much more different than what I was used to before I left the featherdom. How strange this last day has been. Shame I never got to meet Tariq again. I'm certain we could have had many adventures. And what a shame I never actually found out what those growling things were, that travelled the pathways outside. Oh well, I wonder what time it is?* Dave looked at his watch to make a note of the time, just so he may avoid this particular time in his next life, if he ever got one.

That's just excellent, he thought as he was

reminded once more he didn't actually have a watch. *Perhaps I ought to get a watch, but there's probably no point now,* he concluded.

All through his ponderings Dave hadn't noticed he'd completely passed through the apparition as it had screamed through the air towards him. Now, as he gazed straight ahead, Dave felt great relief, albeit for a very short amount of time. The apparition had apparently disappeared. The short amount of time now being over Dave suddenly became aware that he had a more immediate problem.

There was a large white, flat, huge white expanse of white ceiling that he was very certain would not suddenly step aside, all the while saying, '*pass by me, it's my pleasure*' nor was he going to be able to pass through it unless he was extremely lucky. Dave thought that he must have used up all of his luck by now.

He braced himself for a huge impact, once again, certain of his imminent demise.

Oh well, Dave thought to himself. *This seems very familiar*, he added finally.

Chapter 25
Moving Pencil Cases and Exam Failure

After its initial shock the Movitall was quite pleased the brown feather, with its weird suit and gloves, and stuff, had not reduced its momentum; the momentum it was relying on to ensure it could move the pencil case and gain its pass in the GHoST Module 2 exam; the pass that would secure its position as one of the coveted few; a fully-fledged poltergeist.

Onwards and downwards, it thought. The

Movitall readied itself for tackling the pencil case in some extreme momentum powered '*mov-it-ture*' manoeuvre.

It grabbed hold of the pencil case whilst it allowed its body to slip through the top of the chest of drawers in its downward journey. Into the top drawer its legs and bottom half slipped. All the while it kept hold of the blue pencil case; both its arms embracing the denim pen and pencil holdall.

Now push, the Movitall commanded itself.

The Movitall came flying out through the chest's top expecting to suddenly slow down as it kept its grip on the pencil case. But to its amazement this did not happen, for a reason unknown.

What? The Movitall thought as the pencil case came away from the chest top throwing the Movitall into an uncontrolled airborne somersault. The water from the jam jar had caused the glue to become temporarily unstuck.

"Whooaaaa!" the Movitall exclaimed as it went spinning off into the air just like a raw egg would, if it had been thrown.

The Movitall smashed clumsily into a light fitting dangling from the ceiling; it still held the pencil case in its hands.

The pencil case's sudden and unexpected release from the top of the chest of drawers had made the Movitall lose all concentration.

The Movitall shook its head as it considered its failings, but some other influence had a thought about what it could do with the Movitall; gravity had grabbed hold.

"It's alright," Gravity consoled in its gravelly voice, glad to capture another victim. "I've got you!"

"Oh no," the Movitall groaned as it started an unwanted journey towards the floor.

The Movitall was now falling with its back to the floor; the pencil case above it and its hands firmly stuck to the case as the superglue had hardened, once again; the pencil case's breezy journey through the air fanning the glue dry.

As the Movitall made desperate attempts to

remove its hands from the pencil case its flight towards the floor, became more and more ungainly.

Bomp. The floor shuddered as the Movitall hit it.

"Flerr," exhaled the Movitall as the pencil case landed on its stomach.

"Damage, style, control and aggression?" queried the Voice of Mystery from the Netherworld. "Never have I seen such a complete and utter pig's ear made of the four highly held principles, principles that would have entitled you to become a fully-fledged poltergeist, never! You have failed," the Voice of Mystery concluded.

"No, no...," the Movitall wailed. "No?" the Movitall added finally, hoping the last 'no' would change the outcome.

"Never in all my death have I ever seen such a shambles be conducted in the execution of the four principles. Your time is over," the Voice of Mystery said ominously.

"But, but, but," the Movitall said, trying to think of a good reason why it should get a second chance. "It wasn't my fault," the Movitall finished.

"Not your fault? And how so is that?" the Voice of Mystery boomed angrily at the Movitall's impertinence. "Was it not you that grabbed the pencil case?"

This was a difficult point for the Movitall to counter, especially because the pencil case was in plain sight, and still firmly attached to its hands.

"No... I didn't expect you to have an answer," the Voice of Mystery from the Netherworld said. "What has been done shall be undone. For failure is not tolerated nor shall the evidence of failure remain to be seen."

A thin green rotting hand with sharp and dirty black fingernails appeared in the air and pointed at the shaking Movitall.

"From here you shall be gone," the Voice of Mystery boomed.

"Nnnnooooooooo," the Movitall screamed in

horror.

A pus-yellow light leapt from the end of the index finger of the floaty hand of horror, and zapped towards the Movitall.

"Aaarrrghhh," screamed the Movitall shutting its eyes as its very being was reduced, first to a globby bubbling mass and then into a pile of dust finally dissolving away to nothing.

The pencil case twitched, then shivered, then leapt back to where it had started from. The maths books popped out of the unused toilet rolls, unfurled themselves and flapped gracefully from the bathroom back to the shelf in the cupboard, where they had been quite happy until the thing had moved them. The duvet stood up, dusted itself down and *flomped* back on to the bed; pillow retraced its steps and finally the CD player burst into a few bars of 'Bat out of Hell' by Meatloaf, and zoomed back to the chest of drawers.

The hand then seemed to take an infinite breath inwards, shrinking all the while until it *shlopped* out of existence.

"Aaarrggghhh," the Movitall screamed again as it opened its eyes, only to realise it had been sent back to the first class of its last year of Poltergeist University.

"No, no, no," the Movitall continued. "This is purgatory."

"Exactly," said the Voice of Mystery from the

Netherworld, smiling to itself.

"Welcome back, Brian," the Headless Master said as he greeted the returnee. "Let's make sure, next time, you don't return to frequent my lessons."

The Movitall nodded in wholehearted agreement.

Chapter 26
Coracles Are Best

For a while Dave's attention on where he was heading had been distracted. He'd been shocked when the strange and awful voice had given the weird thingamajig a serious telling off.

But he'd been even more shocked when a green, rotting hand had appeared, zapped and evaporated the scary what-d'you-call-it, and then disappeared itself.

But at least he now knew what the problem had been, and what had caused the girls' misery—everything, the moving stuff and the hidden stuff, had been caused by an undergraduate poltergeist, and a thing that was tested on moving stuff to places where the stuff shouldn't be!

What a strange thing to be tested on, Dave thought, and wondered if he'd ever get the hang of his new life. And as the thought passed through his head, he looked up. *OMG!* Dave thought further.

With the ceiling getting so much nearer Dave dismissed ever getting used to his new life. And as he considered there was no point even trying to get used to his new life, he suddenly remembered Tariq's coracle. Quickly he plunged his hand into his pocket and extracted the bright yellow pointy thing.

The ceiling was almost upon him. But he knew he had to remember the time back in Tariq's muddy pen and what had happened. How this yellow thingy had saved him. Dave was desperate, the ceiling was getting closer, very quickly. He just had to remember that simple thing, the one thing that had happened. If not he was doomed to be splatted against the hard flat ceiling.

Dave looked at the yellow thing's flimsy material. He examined its black "J" shaped handle, and the silver point beneath which the coracle's yellow skin was. But nothing seemed to offer a way to make the object change shape, just as it had done in Tariq's pen.

Dave looked closely at the yellow stick's shaft—there was nothing, apart from a small silver defect sticking out from the coracle's cylindrical pole.

Dave glanced at the oncoming ceiling once more, and seeing he was no more than a little bit over a metre from it, he grabbed the coracle's shaft a lot tighter, thinking he may be able to climb down it before he hit the ceiling. But really it was just his reaction to the fear of an almighty splat that would fall upon him—just like an insect against an aeroplane's cockpit. Dave didn't know the same thing could happen to insects against car windscreens, as the cars rushed along the motorways or arterial roads. He hadn't been around long enough to properly know what a car was, or how roads worked. Something sunk beneath his tight grip.

FWOP. The umbrella opened towards the ceiling.

In an instant his speed was reducing. And the ceiling started to stop coming so near, so fast. Then within the blink of an eye Dave started to float back towards the floor, the ceiling all the while moving away from him.

Well I'll be, Dave thought, *well done Tariq... again!*

Yet another item Tariq had given him had

saved the day.

Chapter 27
All's Well That Starts Badly

Dave landed on the girls' blue carpet, and just in time.

GROWL, CLUMP, CRAM.

Dave heard a sound he recognised—it was one of the multi-coloured growling monsters; and it had stopped outside the house, and people had just got out of it, its doors slammed behind them.

Then he heard voices; children talking quietly. The house's front door opened and then shut. The family were back.

The girls' mother was talking. "...and if you ever try that again I will not be happy." Dave heard the girl's mother finish.

Hannah and Josephine ran up the stairs to their bedroom.

Dave had managed to get back to the floor of the room, fold up his coracle, shove it back into one of his impossibly deep pockets, and then sneak back behind the chest of drawers.

The girls sat back on Hannah's bed.

"How are we going to go to the next maths lesson without our books, Han?" Jo asked.

"Jo. We can't go without them. And that is all there is to it."

"But what can we do, Han? Mother expects us to go to the next one because she has paid."

"I know, Jo. But without any pocket money we're just going to get into more trouble. And that's all there is to it." Hannah shook her head.

"Han, did you really, really, really look *really* properly in the cupboard?"

"You know I did. You were with me."

"I know, but we didn't do anything. Our books just went."

"Books don't just go. We must've just forgotten where we put them. That's all."

"Han! I don't remember us putting them anywhere else." Jo was pleading, even more miserable than before. "What are we going to do? We can't afford new ones and Grandma won't give us the money," Jo finished.

Hannah was just about to take her shoes off when she noticed the old tulip stems on the floor. "Oh no!" she said.

"What's the matter, Han?" Jo asked her sister.

Hannah pointed at the dead flowers on the floor. "Look."

"Oh!" Jo said. "Don't worry. I'll clear them up."

"That's not important," Hannah told her sister. "We need to do something about the books."

"I know. But I can't think of anything." Jo

was almost in tears but then added. "Perhaps if we look in the cupboard once more we might see them. It might be that we just didn't see them for looking last time."

"That's stupid, Jo. We've done that twice now. And you think a trip out to the shops and back might make it right?"

"We were away when it happened," Jo replied with a simple logic that couldn't be denied.

"Yeah," Hannah agreed. "I suppose you're right there, you silly one." Hannah brushed Jo's fringe from her face and smiled at her younger sister. "Try not to worry," she said. Sometimes Jo had a way about her that Hannah couldn't but admire.

"Okay. Let's have another look then," Jo said, happy her sister had agreed.

Jo and Hannah went to the cupboard and stood beside it, neither of them wanting to have a look, a look that would prove they were still in terrible trouble. Hannah pulled the cupboard door open once more, slowly this time with her eyes shut.

"Hannah, Hannah, Hannah," Jo exclaimed, jumping up and down jabbing her finger at the open cupboard. "They're there. There they are. The books are there!"

Hannah opened her eyes, thinking Jo was not seeing the truth of the matter. But to Hannah's surprise there they were, just as they'd left them the day before. Hannah shut the door and opened it again, just to make sure. The books, the maths books, were there!

"Yes, Jo, the books are there," Hannah said not knowing what to think. They were saved.

"Jo, are you going to clean up those flowers now? Before Mother comes up?"

Jo looked at the chest of drawers then at the floor. "That stupid cat," she said.

While the girls got the cleaning cloth Dave edged his way out of the room and made for the regular cliff he'd climbed up earlier that day. Down the stairs he went hoping there'd be no more extraordinary forces that would make him levitate until, at least, he got out of the house; but his preference was not to be levitated ever again, unless it was by his own doing.

The girls' mother was busying herself with some things in one of the rooms at the bottom of the stairs, and Dave was able to make his way out of the house, back the way he had come.

He pushed the flap in the kitchen door open and jumped through it. He was out. Quickly Dave made his way to the side passage and crept along the short pathway.

He was pleased, the girls were now okay and although he hadn't solved their problem directly, he felt, with some satisfaction, that he'd been a part of the solution, and how good was that? Dave smiled to himself. He really was the helper of needful people.

Dave pushed open the flap and left, now the girls were okay

Chapter 28
Back to the Beginning

Once back on the cracked path, next to the road, Dave relaxed. He was still feeling quite pleased with himself. But what could he do now? Who could he help next?

I know, I'll go and see Tariq and thank him for all his help, Dave thought.

Dave was certain that without the stuff Tariq had given him; the coracle, the un-X-Ray glasses, he would not have been able to accomplish what he had.

For Dave it was an absolute necessity to thank Tariq; although Tariq hadn't been there to help the girls, he *had* helped. And, perhaps, Tariq would be interested in what had happened.

Only one problem now and that was how he would get across the road without being sucked off his feet.

However, as it turned out, it was not a problem. Darkness was settling in once again and the number of cars rushing up and down the dark pathway was considerably less than earlier that day.

Dave crossed the road and once on the other side he followed the cracked path back to the house, behind which was Tariq's place.

Dave walked down the passageway that ran alongside the house, past the wall of pebbles, and was about to step out of the shadows when he saw a large person standing over Tariq's wooden home.

Dave's mouth dropped open. The huge person had lifted up the roof of Tariq's house. The man was bending over, looking inside for something. Then the man reached in and took handfuls of stuff from Tariq's home and threw it into a big black rubbish sack.

Oh my word! Dave thought. *That man is searching for Tariq! I hope Tariq's okay.* Dave stepped back into the shadows, worried, wondering what he could do to help the kind

person who'd helped him so much earlier.

About the Author

 Simon needed to do something very special for his daughters, for their Christmas present. Although he'd worked in I.T. for over 15 years, at the time, and knew about project planning, what he decided to take on was completely out of his comfort zone and capability, and this fact was to be adequately demonstrated on more than one occasion.

In his naivety, he decided to write a story about a super hero whose only superpower was the fact that he had impossibly deep pockets. Once done Simon would wrap the book up, in amazing Christmas paper, and hand a copy to each of his daughters: this was in February 2003, the goal being to hand the "amazing" present to them around 25th December 2003—and that is where the project totally fell apart.

It took Simon a couple of months to finish writing the story, but as he wanted it to be the best for Molly and Tilly; as any father would, he sent the manuscript to a professional literary agency to garner their opinion. The result; "an original story", and to paraphrase now, "but the writing is crap". Simon was shocked. He'd paid for the analysis and they'd told him it was crap – that's a sure sign of professionalism; the agency had done what they'd been paid for – no sucking up.

Of course, they were right; Simon hadn't been trained, so he embarked on multiple writing courses, including script writing courses, then rewrote the story. By the time he'd completed this endeavour he'd missed Christmas 2003 by 18 months! But he continued simply because it is his philosophy that if you don't do anything to achieve your goal, you'll never achieve your goal.

Now he has an agent. It has been a long and

informative journey for Simon; somewhat echoing Brave Dave's journey of learning, but he's pleased to acknowledge the journey hasn't finished yet. With three more novels in the series complete, and two others in the wings, he's certain you'll have enjoyed this first story, as it describes the beginnings of Brave Dave's education in the world of women, men, children and beasts.

<u>More in the Brave Dave series</u>;

The Time Goblin

The Caribbean Conspiracy

A Space Oddity

www.BraveDave.co.uk

www.srwoodward.co.uk

Twitter:

@srwoodwardUK

Facebook:

https://www.facebook.com/srwoodwarduk

www.ingramcontent.com/pod-product-compliance
Lightning Source LLC
Chambersburg PA
CBHW031222120726
47905CB00002B/440